MARBLE SKIN

W·W·NORTON & COMPANY
NEW YORK · LONDON

MARBLE SKIN

A NOVEL

TRANSLATED FROM THE
FRENCH BY GREG MOSSE

SLAVENKA
DRAKULIĆ

Printed in the United States of America
Manufacturing by The Haddon Craftsmen, Inc.

ISBN 0-393-03477-1

W. W. Norton & Company, Inc.
500 Fifth Avenue, New York, N.Y. 10110
W. W. Norton & Company Ltd.
10 Coptic Street, London WC1A 1PU

1 2 3 4 5 6 7 8 9 0

1

Suddenly it happened.

I thought I had already forgiven my mother for everything.

I was at a private view when a woman friend asked me why all my sculptures of the female body seemed eaten away inside. Although the hollowness can't be seen, you feel it, somewhere, just beneath the marble skin. Yes, that's what she called it, the 'marble skin', even though I have rarely worked in marble, just a few small statues. I have always avoided it. My material is wood. I remember she gestured with her hand as if to brush against this imaginary skin and her two silver bracelets slipped down her thin wrist

1

and tinkled against one another. The metallic sound and the strange words echoed in the half-empty gallery where the painter NB was showing large floral, pastel canvases. The assertion surprised me. Its formulation, in such contrast with the paintings, confused me. I had to look away, at the pale, matt-brown parquet. I answered that I had not known that the emptiness remained visible despite everything. Of course, I only wanted to surround it, not to fill it. 'Which would be impossible,' I added, as if in justification. And against my will I began to talk about symbols, overt structures and the metaphorical meaning of forms – clichés you normally encounter flowing from the pens of critics.

I tried to explain to her that I did not like the hardness of marble. My sculptures are 'dark forms' in wood, clay or terracotta – great abstract shapes the colour of loam, sand or burnt wood. I had sculpted a few marble nudes, but only, I thought, as an exercise, to prove to myself I could master such a cold, hard medium and overcome the repulsion it inspired in me. But then, in the gallery, prompted by my friend's observations and my explanations, I could see that these sculptures, these women's bodies, were completely different from everything else I had done. I felt the words were coming too easily out of my mouth and stopped speaking.

2

How could I tell her, how could I make her understand with words what a woman's body is?

The next day I went to the studio. It was an afternoon in summer. In a corner a pile of recently-dug clay covered with wet rags exhaled its perfume. I tore off a lump and dug my fingers into it so violently that it hurt the quicks of my nails. The clay was still raw, irregular. Kneading it I warmed it up till it was totally submissive and would take the imprint of the tiniest lines on my palm. Cool clay resisting at first; allowing myself to relax in the silence; little pink honeysuckle leaves round the window . . . For the first time in ages I felt I could dare to summon the image which torments me.

But why do they always emerge together, the image of the mother and the image of the body? Why, when I think body, do I always see only her, lying in the darkened bedroom, her left arm out straight and her head resting upon it, her lips half open and her dark hair dishevelled? It obscures part of her face and neck, as if smothering her. She lies naked on the edge of the bed, on her side, her legs slightly bent. It is hot. Outside the wooden shutters reigns a summer like today's, dry and dusty. In the shaft of grainy yellow light I recognise from afar the soft curve of her belly, her small round breasts with their pale nipples, the roundness of her hips, her shoulders and knees on which the afternoon sun lingers.

I seem to touch her, the clay is already so hot.

As if brushing my hand across her breasts, damp from that stuffy room, damp from sleep.

Tension mounts inside within me. I want to come closer, to hold myself against her. Dive into her body like the sea. I am already so close that I can distinguish the tiny drops of sweat on her forehead. I catch the familiar, captivating smell of her hair. But from her other side another hand, a man's hand, reaches towards her, toward her belly. In her sleep she rolls onto her back and slowly opens her legs to give him room.

My hands, abandoned, knead the clay.

Its stickiness fills me with helplessness and disgust.

I knew that this time I could do nothing worthwhile with clay, not even a maquette. It is too weak a medium. It has no resistance. Working clay, you can change your mind and remodel it, and that allows a kind of tenderness. Perhaps I could have painted her, catching her in one of her thousands of moments, slowly turning over for example. Yes, that would definitely have been interesting. I could have created a closed system, an internal tension, stability in the skin colour. But as soon as I closed

4

my eyes her painted body would have turned into just one more crass canvas, its smooth surface roughened by layers of paint.

What I wanted was a fullness of form, to be able with closed eyes to touch her breasts and feel their excitement flow back towards me. To establish contact between two substances, two aspects of reality whose presence fills the space around them.

I also knew that I didn't need to prepare myself in any way. I had to attack the material straight away, grasp the bend of her knee, the way she rolled over in her sleep to give herself. This inaccessible sleeping body required stone, hard like the image it left in me. Something into which I could drive my chisel and wrench out the shape I wanted, before the body-vision, once more drifting on the edge of consciousness, could sink back into memory, becoming an integral part of me once more.

Still unfinished, vulnerable, I open her legs with a single blow of my hammer, being careful not to touch the vein of the stone. Then work long and hard on the contours to obtain exactly the right curve – the taut bow running from the thigh to the toes, through the knee. The most enjoyable part of the work would be the polishing, sensitive fingertips feeling out and exploring the smallest hollows and bumps, judging their relationship,

5

their harmony, the finesse with which they melt into one another.

A contact only permitted me, my hand alone, at last.

To forget one's own body. Not to forget it.

My teacher, the sculptor AM, in her studio at the Visual Arts Academy, leaning on the wall of dirty ochre brick. She is talking about dead sculptures, about the body. 'How can you sculpt a human being if you are incapable of feeling your own body and the space around it? We don't *have* a body, we *are* a body.' Having said this she grabbed my arm just above the elbow and squeezed so hard that tears came into my eyes. 'Don't you see,' she said, pushing a finger at a plaster cast of a man's torso, 'that this is dead, that it doesn't interact with the space around it? It's dead,' she added sadly, releasing me and pacing to and fro, her hands thrust deep into the pockets of her white coat. She might have been referring to the death of a friend.

Yes, but to feel one's body is painful.

Straightaway I started work, that very same summer two years ago. Outside in the courtyard adjoining my studio the block of marble rang like a bell. I worked obsessively. Dust and splinters bit into my skin, my vocal cords, my lungs. I could have chosen an easier medium. If I had wanted to sculpt

6

any woman's body – not *her* body – wood would have been much more suitable. It requires less physical effort. It is more malleable, is easier to manipulate and allows a certain carelessness. My hand is used to wood, recognising and easily mastering it.

Or I could have chosen pink alabaster which can be carved as easily as wood. Slightly lighter alabaster on the surface (the transparency of skin), darker in the centre (her concentrated, dark red desire). But only marble provided enough resistance. Only through physical effort, by mastering my medium, could I bring out into the open what she had spent her whole life hiding from me: passion. And as I worked the space around her filled with a repulsive energy, what AM called 'negative space'.

I had to decide on the scale I would use for her. Before ordering the block of flesh-coloured marble, I already thought she should be larger than life – I would have to step back in order to take her in completely in one glance. To be able to hold her in my hands – to squeeze her tight – to reduce her: then that would have been the true measure of the statue. Then I would have almost entirely possessed her. Not altogether though. Marble has its firmness, its density, its resistance, that it is dangerous to try and disregard. But immediately I felt it would be impossible to reduce her: her size still crushed me, this mass of stone looming out of the past dominated the little girl of fourteen, blocking her view.

Her closeness, the distance.

The cold skin between us.

Eventually there she was, lying on the bed, like in the image which torments me. I could approach her, right up close. Touch her. She no longer escaped me. I gazed at her, her head thrown back, her face, her fine, straight nose with its quivering nostrils, her full, half-open lips – I felt that at any moment she might sigh and shrug off the weight of my gaze from her breasts.

She was so submissive that the eye melted over her curves, forgetting they were stone . . . Her marble skin was not highly polished, shining. I did not want her to be too smooth to the touch, too slippery – one's hand should have time to memorise the form. She seemed to have goose flesh, her cold skin bristling with tiny invisible hairs. Outside it was already the beginning of winter.

She lay there peacefully. As if waiting for something. For that hand again. For his hands. For all of him.

Complete and perfect, confident of her captivating beauty – of which I was a prisoner. For a while I let her rest down at the end of the studio, under the sloping glass roof with its cloak of ivy. In the green shadow, like in a wood, she slept calmly, innocently, until the leaves had fallen and the limpid blue light of the autumn sky drenched her through the dry twigs. When I came close to her once more and saw her in that harsh light – her form standing out sharply against the dark background – I knew the time had come for us to strip ourselves completely naked. To rid myself once and for all of the weight of this body I carried around inside me.

When I exhibited her, her sensuality was like a challenge. Visitors couldn't help touching her and, after a few days, the dirty fingermarks left on her body made me nauseous, but a strange excitement gripped me at the thought of all these people doing what I had never been able to do, at the thought of the forbidden gesture.

I stood to one side as the gallery emptied. A young man passed close by her. As he reached the door he turned right round as if he had forgotten something. She lay on a low plinth, almost at floor level, with her legs half spread and her hand in between. The space around her throbbed with an inner tension: her aroused desire. He leaned over and placed his hand on hers. I could see him from where I stood, in his black overcoat, as he bent his back and spread his fine white fingers over her hand, until he completely encompassed it.

I was dumbfounded, shaken – by the touch of this hand that I lightly but unequivocally felt on me. At that moment I knew I had not yet forgiven her.

We had not yet managed to distance ourselves sufficiently from one another, still I was her.

I had given the sculpture its only possible title: *My Mother's Body*. That caused a stir, letters to the press, a debate of sorts. One critic talked of cruelty, of revenge; another of the New Woman and the authenticity of desire. Still another wrote that the statue could only have been sculpted by a man's, by a lover's hand.

If only there had not been that word: mother.

Without it the violent desire I had revealed – the obsession with her own gratification on which her whole being concentrated, even as she slept – would not have been so unsettling. Along with her passion, from the depths of her stone guts a sort of fluid flowed, a kind of opaque, unpleasant mystery. But her so pure beauty erased everything.

Having seen a photograph of it published filling almost a quarter of a page, my mother, who lives in another town, tried to end it all.

She had not understood that by wrenching it out from the very deepest part of me I had made her beauty a reality.

She very nearly succeeded.

'She will sleep for a long time,' said the doctor as he gave her an injection. 'She is very weak.'

He was still young but already a little bald. He did not try to hide it by dragging his hair forward. That seemed to me reason enough to take what he said seriously. He looked at me. His eyes lingered on my face a little too long and I began to tremble. He must have seen in my eyes what separated us, her and me, all the time gone by between her two suicide attempts, estranging us.

Time. Ice.

It was long ago, so long ago. In her room, in front of the mirror, stood a little crystal chest containing biscuits. I thought my mother was asleep. Very softly, so as not to wake her, I lifted the lid and licked my right forefinger to pick up the sugar and crumbs at the bottom. As I sucked my finger, gazing at the porcelain ballerina standing in front of the mirror, I was first struck by the smell. Acrid, alarming, alcohol, hospital corridors, the unknown. In a corner of the mirror, right next to the figurine, I saw her hand, hanging, almost touching the ground. Only then did I notice she was moaning – suddenly her breathing stopped and her lungs seemed to be gathering their strength to overcome some invisible obstacle. Neither the sight of her nor her sobs frightened me. But I stayed rooted to the spot at the thought that I had crossed the whole bedroom, as far as the biscuit box, without turning round. If she suddenly woke from her anguished suicidal slumber she would know that I sometimes entered her room without permission.

I leaned slightly to the right. In the oval mirror I could now see all of her double bed with its carved headboard, the night table, the lighted lamp and the chair over which she had draped her black silk dressing gown. Because of the way she was lying her face was invisible. I thought she might be crying, that I shouldn't look at her, that she would resent it. She was wearing a pink, short-sleeved nightdress, the front decorated with lace and a row of little round mother-of-pearl buttons. I felt there was a contradiction between these brilliant white pearls, the uneven pink lacework and her hand hanging out of the bed. I stopped sucking my finger.

Then as if, though only a child, I had been given a complete overview of the orchestration of all things, of life itself, I saw the bedroom one warm evening, in the fading light of a lamp with a glass shade turned towards the wall and shadows on the floor, I recognised the familiar smell of clean linen carefully put away in the cupboard as its fragrance filtered out and slowly rose towards me . . . I knew she was safe.

It was only then, I think, that I recognised this particular kind of swoon, that I gave it a name, that

I recognised suicide by its smell. A sudden shiver at the word 'death', then relief.

In that pink nightdress – no, it's completely impossible.

The image of her distant suicide attempt, as it remained in my memory, was so tender, edged with lace and dim light, that I sometimes felt that it was a scene from a play in which she was starring. A beautiful, long-haired woman, on the edge of eternity, adorned as if the death that stalked her was the lover she had long awaited.

'I think everything will be all right,' I said, watching the doctor open his leather instrument case to swallow the folded stethoscope.

He nodded.

'Let's hope so,' he replied. 'She isn't completely out of danger.'

Cold gripped me as I entered the house this evening after eighteen years' absence. The difference in temperature between outside (warm, early autumn) and inside chilled me to the bone. The sudden cold, welcoming and rejecting at the same time, rubbed against my skin, abruptly absorbing its warmth. In the glazed entrance hall everything was transparent. Not a shadow, not one dark corner: harsh white walls merged invisibly with the white-paved floor. I took several steps with my gaze lowered, as if at any moment I risked slipping up on so much whiteness.

The kitchen is a large, slightly darker room with a window overlooking the courtyard; black and white tiles, a big old oven and shelves of china pots containing flour, sugar, salt, semolina, coffee and cinnamon; on the table in the centre, a narrow-necked vase; in the vase, a completely-wilted tulip. I poured the water down the sink. A smell of decay was released, alone in the odourless room. There were no cooking smells here, unlike other kitchens, no smell of garlic, of frying, of apple tarts or stews.

In her kitchen smells disappeared quickly, as if driven out.

The food she cooked was real, all the same; soups, courgettes *au gratin*, pickled fish, stuffed peppers. She spent ages kneading cake mixes. Yes, she did all that. But she didn't like anyone to see her doing it.

As soon as we had finished eating the table was cleared – the smooth white porcelain crockery gave the food the appearance and sheen of plastic – and the washing up had to be done without delay.

She would put the vase back on the table as if hiding all trace of her inner weakness. She changed the white linen napkins that she kept in large wooden napkin rings decorated with a swan for the smallest coffee stain, for the tiniest smear of yolk from our boiled eggs. She changed everything – the napkins and towels, the sheets, the drying-up cloths – in silence, almost furtively, as if in silent reproach. One day when we had guests someone knocked over a glass of wine: she stood up and removed the tablecloth with a smile. But I remember noticing the accelerated pulsing of a small vein in her neck. I saw her resisting, with an enormous effort restraining herself from dashing into the kitchen for salt to spread on the stain, rubbing it hard with her fingers until it turned dark blue, her whole being ached to make the stain disappear. I saw her carefully remove the tablecloth and use a corner of it to absorb the puddle of spilt wine: red on white.

She hated stains. They pained her.

I saw her suffer. The pain condensed and locked itself away inside her. I would have liked to have made those gestures, wiping the table for her, making sure the wine didn't drip on the carpet. I got up, ready to help her. I touched her wet hand. She looked at me as if I was trying to deprive her of something which was hers by right. As if I was incapable of understanding what it was all about. I can still remember the slightly vinegary smell of the spilt wine, as the guests continued their conversation without noticing her bewilderment, her life suddenly sullied by billowing red stains, unable to conceal her agitation from strangers.

And now everything is calm in the kitchen, as if nothing had ever happened here. From the point where I now stand, where the tiles meet the parquet, as if I had never returned to her all the hatred of the body that she had drilled into me over the years.

In the living room the roller shutters were, as usual, half closed. Light filtered lacily through the narrow oak strips, condensing in short, slender beams glowing filigree on the rug. Its brightness pierced my eyes like shards of glass. The light was superfluous here, hostile. It brings objects out into the open, revealing their nakedness. I noticed that the wallpaper had faded, that the diagonal lines separating the rustic floral patterns, once dark red, were now a dirty brown. The whole room seemed cloaked in a film of grey smoke. It seemed the furniture was losing its shape, that the angles had been rounded off, that the whole room had become oval. Here and there squares were torn from the fine smoke curtain and a lemon yellow background appeared like blue sky seen through clouds. The tiny, delicate flowers suddenly regained their freshness as when the paper was new. 'She is hiding something,' I said to myself as my hand felt round the edge of an empty square.

The nausea overwhelmed me and I started: the photographs!

There used to be photographs. Their absence still clung so determinedly to the wall that the effect was practically the same: the photographs were there, just under the lighter patches. I knew that if I waited a little they would reappear.

In front of her bedroom door I halted with a feeling of *déjà vu*. My body recognised the worn wooden threshold and the large, rounded architrave as I rested my forehead against it, already weary of gouging my way through the thick composite of the past. Before even touching the door handle my hand drew back, giving in to anxiety. In the shining brass, at the point where the handle curved, I saw a kind of warning. No, not yet. Do not open this door, wait a little.

Anxiety makes me shrink. I am now so small that I can see what I used to call the handle's bottom. A secret place. Dark, dirty perhaps. Just underneath, the lock. She thinks that I am peeping through the keyhole. She accuses me, her voice cutting the air in the stuffy corridor, precluding all explanation. I want to tell her that . . . but she is gone. I am left alone in front of the door she slams and behind which she disappears. Behind which she is now resting.

Still today I am afraid to enter.

I would hear a door close behind me, the furtive noise of a key in the lock, then footsteps.

Silence and a man's footsteps. Coming closer.

A moment which was to cut my life in two.

I went in all the same. Only the presence of the others – the doctor and the nurse – enabled me to cross the threshold. The room was dark. The nurse had draped a scarf over the already-dim lamp. In the diffuse light I had trouble seeing the outline of the furniture, but I knew it by heart. Nothing had changed in the house, in her room, these eighteen years, as if not a single object had been moved. How much dust must have settled in all that time! She must have carefully lifted each knick-knack from its place to dust it, before gingerly putting it back. Like a cleaning woman in a museum of antique furniture ... The silence which reigns in the stale air enclosed by the apartment's sealed windows is not the only thing that calls to mind a museum.

I have goose flesh at the thought that I too remember the precise location of every exhibit in that museum.

I approached the bed and furtively kissed her forehead. Her face seemed unreal, like a thin, paper mask. Her pale, delicate skin was stretched across her cheekbones, almost blue and transparent on her forehead. In the hollows of her eyes it was lined, thickened and swollen. I noticed for the first time that she had no eyebrows left, just a few scarcely visible hairs. She replaced the prominent curve that used to slope down towards her eyelid with a thin brown pencil line. A gaze without eyebrows, without lashes.

Beneath that membrane she slept. Motionless. Silent. Equally distant.

She was about to raise her eyelids, hesitating, and look at me. 'Give me a minute to pull myself together,' she said. She just daubed on some lipstick. Energetically, determinedly, as if, each day, she practised self-recognition. She never gave up – as if it was her way of delineating a frontier not to be crossed, however she might feel at the time. 'I feel naked without make-up,' she'd said. I smile with surprise, because never, never had I seen her naked. For a moment I feel a sudden itching in my hands to do just that, to snatch away the sheet. But just looking at her sleeping face made me want to cry: grave, her expression etched with sadness and reproach.

Within and without, so well defined for her, irreconcilable.

Without now withering her skin.

She is going to wake up, I thought, and feel me looking at her, like a wet poultice on her face. She must have been sleeping alone for a long time now, no one there to gaze, before she falls asleep, on her still-perfect bone structure, so well-preserved beneath her rice-paper skin protecting her from all danger. She no longer opens the bedroom window wide. She no longer has the strength, as she used to, to expose her sheets, her privacy, her face, her everything to the sun.

My child's eye examining this adult face, climbing the vertical of time until the present moment – until me leaning over her, aware of my power.

'She shouldn't be left alone,' said the doctor, looking at me once more.

'No, of course, I shall stay with her,' I hastened to reply, far too quickly.

As if I was frightened of myself, as if afraid I was capable of abandoning her. The knot of guilt in my stomach tightened into a hard ball. The doctor frowned and said nothing. I felt he didn't trust me – perhaps because of my unconvincing tone. The nurse pulled the covers up to her chin. As they stood in the doorway the scarf slipped from the lamp and I saw my mother's white face flattening, merging into the sheet. Again I thought of decomposition, of death, as I had condemned her that day in the kitchen, hating her helplessness.

I had told her: 'I wish you were dead!'

My voice erupted from my guts. Inside I felt it as a whine.

Outside it echoed like a snarl.

20

She was astonished. Then, painfully, she let herself slip down into a chair, both hands grasping the edge of the table. Like someone ageing suddenly, becoming embarrassed of their body, of themselves.

She already moved as if she had been annihilated. Perhaps in that moment she understood how much I wished her dead – a complete, definitive renunciation of her.

'No, no, I'll stay with her,' I said once more, shutting the door behind them.

I had to close it. When they had gone I could no longer stand to look at that scene: the room, the bed, her.

Here we are again alone together in the house. The night is cool and humid with a distant sound of crickets coming from the park. My mother is asleep on the far side of the wall. I am lying tight up against it, touching it with my knees. As I fall into sleep a strange feeling of lack, of absence, of carefully emptied space swells inside me.

The way things slowly dry out, the way the house withdraws into its shell.

This room, 'my room', is smaller than when I left it. It gives the impression of everything being piled up, squeezed in. I feel I can touch the ceiling with my hand, the gold paper frieze and the round

21

crystal chandelier. Everything is in its place: the bed to the right, the wardrobe to the left, the old leather armchair, the table, the lamp, the shelves in between. Only the wallpaper is new. Perhaps she intends to take in a lodger. On the wall opposite me at one point the strips of wallpaper are badly aligned, making the whole room look crooked. The perspective seems broken, the space unknown and neutral – like a hotel room. Sudden feeling of imbalance, dizziness.

Then, just as sudden, relief: it is good to feel taken out of context, even if only because of the wallpaper. I finally notice some photographs above my bed, where in a hotel room an engraving of the town or a bleak landscape in a cheap iron frame would hang. The wall seems totally covered. Each photograph is of me.

In the first, the smallest, just above the pillow, she is holding me in her arms in the courtyard of a house by the sea. She wears a printed piquet dress. Her shoulder-length hair is held by a white ribbon. She is so thin that it seems impossible that the package resting on her right arm can be her two-month old baby. The next photograph is of me alone and is a little larger: already I can sit on a wicker armchair on the terrace. In the third I am about four and appear to be leaning on the edge of the photograph. My head is tilted down a little, my face serious, surrounded by stiff blond hair. I am looking, warily, at the camera. The shutter opened a little too soon and my body tense with the effort of keeping my balance. Today the photograph still gives the impression that the little girl is about to start shivering, trembling with something she cannot express. I stretch my hand outside the frame, towards someone very close but retreating, leaving me alone teetering on the edge of the void.

Beyond the photograph the child's hand touched emptiness.

Then the shutter: click!

I recognise the low wall over which she holds me, her brown arms. I fight as she lifts me up. Beyond, the precipice. Far below I can just make out the sea, the cypress trees planted alongside. But I can't look away quickly enough from these distant spaces, concentrate on where I am. I can't ignore the distant sea and follow the narrow, slippery wall with my sandals. I am too small.

I tell her I can't. I shout that I can't, that I am going to fall, that I am falling.

And she laughs. I see her white smile, distant, so distant. She says something in reply but her arms are still crossed on her chest. Bright red nail varnish.

Between us, stone slabs. Between them a few stalks of grass. Sole confirmation of the reality of my existence. I remember my body fighting, the sound of her voice – not what she said. I remember my tense body, the effort I make to hang on to her hand, the fear I feel of the void behind me. At the same time the sound of her voice, unceasing. Like a murmur: soft, very soft. Inexorably soft. Her voice, her voice completely surrounds me. Today still I feel incapable of understanding the words she breathes, the whispering softness, as I allow myself to sink.

Her tricky, commanding, hypnotising voice.

Above it, beneath it, the softness.

Velvet murmur of dark, hot, mysterious water.

Why did she do that?

She took the photographs out of the old album. She had to unstick them. Some came unglued as she turned the pages – I hear the rustle of the fine paper that separates the leaves of card. Turning the photographs over she saw, on the yellowed backs, spots of brownish glue as if that glue alone was holding the past together. Then she had them framed. Only mine. The smallest in oval frames of silver, already patinaed by time spent in a shop window. Finally she had to hang these twenty photographs over my (old) bed in my (old) room, being careful to respect their chronology. The dates were written in green ink on the backs of the pictures.

How much time did she spend in this bedroom? Did she come in every day? Or was she happy to inspect it once a month, gingerly opening the door as if I was still living there?

In the last photograph, in the right-hand corner, I am wearing a swimsuit – my first real one-piece swimsuit. It was blue with a yellow flap across my chest. I hold my arms folded awkwardly, as if I am trying to hide my breasts. They cannot yet be seen – at least not from the outside. But I know they are there. I feel them already, small, hard pads, painful around the nipple. I am eleven. The sequence ends there.

Why did she do that?

The faces watch me, unsmiling, serious, multiple reflections of myself. That is how she sees me. How she wants to see me for ever. Under glass. Miniatures of a little blond girl who must never, ever grow up.

I climb on the bed and take down the photographs one by one. Calmly, with an absence of emotion which worries me. I do not dare put them on the floor for fear of breaking them, of crushing beneath my heel this row of frames whose sequence halts abruptly on the brink of the abyss. I unhook them gently so as not to wake her. Not a speck of dust, not even on the tops of the highest frames. Museum of absence, dumbness, screaming silence.

Where the wallpaper is poorly aligned I try to tear off a piece and scratch the plaster. I want to rip away the layers of time that have accumulated between this child and the woman I have become. The wallpaper holds; I feel its hostility through my fingers. It is covered by an invisible film, which resists, which separates us.

Which protects us from one another.

She must have taken the photographs out of the living room beforehand. Four family portraits in gilt oval frames, an enlargement of her at ten years old wearing a dress with a sailor's collar, her marriage photograph and the sole picture of my father.

Next the reflection of the bare yellow wall in her eyes.

My father died before I was three. She, in a fit of despair, anger, contempt or madness – perhaps all of these ('He abandoned me,' she would say when referring to his death) – burnt all the photographs showing them together. At least that is what she told me. All except the photograph hung in the living room, taken at the Milcinski Studio when I was one. My father was forty-three at the time, with a narrow face and brown hair receding at his temples. He smiled into space. His glasses hid a little the melancholy expression in his eyes, in contrast with his barely-formed, almost absent smile, the meditative air with which he looked at the world, his wife and himself and the pain secreted around his mouth like sediment; he let events carry him along and suffered for it.

Events were to get the better of him. He already knew this on the day he went to the photographer's studio.

I begged her to let me put the photograph in my room. She told me the dead were dead, and that was that. I didn't dare ask her what she meant by 'and that was that'. She rarely mentioned him, and always with a repressed bitterness tightening her throat. I said nothing. I was afraid of her blurting it all out onto me. 'He was mad,' she raged. No doubt she thought that he had been dead long enough for her to have the right to dismiss him as a lunatic.

Later, when we had moved out of the house we rented on the outskirts of the city, I met a neighbour from our old road (her husband was managing director of the zoo). Thinking I was bound know what she meant, she referred to 'our tragedy'. That is how I discovered that my father had hung himself in the toolshed at the bottom of the garden and wasn't found until three days later.

It was winter. People looked everywhere, except there.

'It was because of her,' the neighbour told me. 'She was so much younger than him.' She shrugged her shoulders, seeming to consider this ample reason for killing oneself. Evening fell in the street where we stood. I was peeling roast chestnuts. I crushed a shell between my fingers, crushed it to powder.

I looked at my hand: it was completely black. The chestnuts tasted of soot.

'They taste of soot,' said the neighbour, awkwardly.

When we parted she waved to me with both hands for a long while. As if she knew we would never meet again.

During our conversation I felt nothing. I imagined my mother walking behind the coffin dressed in her widow's weeds with a hat and a heavy black veil obscuring her face. She lifts a corner with her lace-gloved hand and dabs her eyes with a handkerchief. White face under the veil. Naked, bright red lips, exposed for a moment to lascivious eyes.

I think black must have suited her.

Now I see my father again. He is standing by the bedroom door. He speaks. His voice is dangerous, like a weapon. He does not want to hurt her but he does. He stabs her in the back with a word. She tries to escape. I see her sitting on the edge of the bed, her face hidden in her hands; she is crying. She shakes her head and repeats: 'No, no, no.'

He reproaches. He threatens. He is tall and wears a dark suit (the blue pinstripe dinner jacket in which he was found) – a dark shadow on the threshold of the beyond. She doesn't turn round, doesn't look at him, merely repeats her denial with a slow shake of the head.

He falls silent and looks at her naked shoulders, soaking up the golden glow of her skin.

The colour of futility.

If she would only turn round, approach him, surely he would stay.

Perhaps she doesn't know this yet. She does not move.

Only tonight – this night – do I seem able to understand the nature of his renunciation: it was impossible to live with her because of the terrorism of her beauty, her flesh, the line of her shoulders, the smell of her hair.

Did she know then the strain of sharing her existence?

She is going to wake up now. She will slide through a crack in the wall and tell me everything at last. The past will stretch out in front of me like a great plain, like a bolt of transparent cloth, and everything will become easy.

'Everything.' That is, the body, hers and mine.

She will talk about our women's bodies. About men: how do they feel to your hand, to your tongue? Does she like what they do? Why is their touch sometimes unbearable? She will say a few words about the things strewn about the house after they leave – their clothes, rough to the touch, not supple like ours.

Perhaps she will also talk about her helplessness, the enchantment which made her melt under their gaze in the street. (My hand will drop hers at that point.) She will describe her distress, the furtive glance down at me: had her little girl noticed her excitement?

In front of men she also referred to me in the third person, as if I wasn't there or as if I was invisible.

She will explain my milk-white fear. I will interrupt her, in the middle of a sentence perhaps. If she will be good enough to listen I will tell her that, despite all the years gone by, I know nothing about men.

Their love is ponderous, impossible, never quite reaching the solitude that is slowly devouring me.

She kept silent to protect me. I grew up in a room with frosted glass walls lined with cotton wool. Through them I could make out only vague shadows, mysterious noises, the terrifying outside world. Still today I do not feel I have ever completely left that room, left myself.

I was going to put the photographs on the top shelf of the double-door wardrobe. I stop myself in the act of turning the key as if forewarned of something: perhaps that's where she has tidied away the sweet papers hidden between the pages of books, the foil from bars of chocolate, the twisted hanks of dodder, the Christmas decorations, the red ribbons with angled ends that she tied in my hair, the open-lace gloves, the pillowcase with a little embroidered bear, a packet of mothballs.

This unfinished childhood is going to tumble down on top of me now, bury me beneath an avalanche of objects she has jealously guarded for thirty-two years. I will disappear once and for all, suffocated by this garbage looming up out of the past, barricading all escape.

She bound me. She blocked my eyes and my ears. She gagged me. Trusting, I accepted all her prohibitions.

As my fingertips trace the tiny round holes in the worm-eaten wood a feeling of disgust wells up inside me and I become completely aware of my hands once more. I feel their weight, their volume, their skin, their slightest movement, their smallest pores, their tiniest nerves. It's as if I'd been absent for a long time. For me they are living, individual beings – bony, rough, calloused in places with short nails encrusted with plaster that no end of scrubbing can quite remove.

All that the surrounding darkness made invisible, I felt with my hands, hard and sensitive at the same time. Later I used them to express the inexpressible. She didn't know that my hands became my only issue from my child's tomb. Running them along the wall of our house I would pick out lumps of plaster. As it flaked away between my fingers I felt happiness, I felt I held my own existence. The worn handle on the tram, the wooden fence, the concave stone steps, balls of bread, clay. It was with my hands and fingers that I learnt to recognise the resistance of matter, its submission, its warmth, its refusal, its repulsion, its desire . . . I knew that touching was a kind of looking, probing objects and people.

Finally I open the wardrobe and my hands lose themselves in the black net of her evening gown. An image seeps out into my fingertips from the depths of my flesh, clear and distinct like an orange glowing in the dark.

I do not need eyes to know which dress it is, with its wide satin skirt and three layers of pleated net, powdered with silver points. Its bodice left her back and shoulders completely naked. Dancing on the terrace that summer evening, she span so fast that

I saw her satin skirt clinging to her body then slowly rising, uncovering her slim calves that reminded me of fish. I thought she would get dizzy and fall. I told her so but she was happy just to glide over to our table near the balustrade and, elated, swallow the mouthful of raspberry squash in the bottom of my glass.

I watched her spin, disappear among the dancers, following her silver sparkling dress with my gaze.

I should have got up. I should have held her hand, not let her go back to the podium, not let her go. But I didn't see him straight away. Something hid him from me, perhaps, as the sea breeze brushed the palm trees ranged among the tables in green wooden planters. Much later I remembered that she had danced only with him, this man in a sky blue shirt. He never came near our table. It was she who got up whenever the music started to play – probably some tango or other – and crossed the dance floor. Then she came back, carried on wings of song. I must have been tired. I didn't understand what it meant at first – the way she wove through the tables, her happiness, her exultation which looked like drunkenness.

Then the man's hand on her shoulder.

She bent her neck and clung to him.

This didn't bother me. But a little later, when they came over to me, I felt that something was wrong. That some very precise threat hung over me: his hand had slipped lower. I saw his hand disappear beneath her bodice, touching her back.

Under the bodice of my dress.

Suddenly I feel them on my skin, those urgent fingers seeking the small of my back. Hot and excited as if scalded by the contact with my flesh beneath the muslin gown. I surrender to their slow caress. He holds me more and more tightly, hard up against him, my breasts grasped by their black tulle, now touching his shirt. I can still hear the two fabrics rubbing against each other, the scarcely-audible sound of two bodies moving. Silver points come away and stick to his clothes. When he gets home he will throw his shirt over the back of a chair and the sparkling points will fall to the carpet.

They will shine there all night, like glow worms.

My breathing slows as if the tense desire crouching inside my expectant body is suffocating me. I become limp, sinking in a red mist on the edge of unconsciousness.

He will realise I'm letting go, giving up already. The sweat on my upper lip will give me away.

No, no, no.

I suck in air and manage to get my breath back, to regain my composure. I see the top buttons of his shirt are undone: I slide my tongue into the opening.

His skin is smooth, salty like an oyster.

The desire to swallow him invades me like a hot tide welling up from my guts into my heart. I have to eat. I must chew up this sweet, viscous flesh beneath the cloth, beneath the skin. While it is still fresh, smelling of seawater and shingle.

My desire propels me to the edge of the dance floor, between two blooming oleander bushes. There I stop spinning and, in the silence awaiting the band's next number, I bite his neck, his shoulder, his biceps.

He tastes salty.

He says nothing. Steps back a little. His hands slowly lower the straps of the bodice and rummage under the brassière.

My naked breasts, exposed to the night and the sea air and spray. I look at him. His hand appears in the shadow of the shrub and reaches out. Touches the nipples. His fingers surround them, harder and harder, as if he wanted to tear them off. The band starts up again and we dance among the oleander once more. A distant street lamp illuminates my naked breasts.

The taste of his skin in my mouth is so bitter that I have to drink two glasses of water to rinse it out. When they came back to the table. I wanted to tell him something: that I had touched him, that I had tasted him. I did nothing but we shook hands and I held on to his longer than necessary.

I thought I could still feel the imprint of her nipple on his palm.

I didn't sleep for long. I awoke in the middle of the night in cold, damp sheets. Beneath me, a stain.

It could only be blood.

The previous evening when I made the bed, the sheet yellow from too long spent in the wardrobe, seeing the crease from the iron, deep in my womb I felt a tickling sensation. Something moving, stinging. It was a sign. I should have guessed and done something to avoid dirtying the linen and the striped mattress ticking. Sometimes when I am tired or travelling I have my period early. But I didn't have time to prepare. I didn't know that my return would transform itself into this nightmare exploration of the past.

Worse: the assault of the past is like the awakening of a long-dormant illness.

It did not cross my mind that my body would react as if it was being physically attacked.

Nevertheless I should have understood as I took my first steps inside the house. My return to the world I had tried to forget for so long could not be painless, unhindered. Without this fear lurking in my abdomen, cupped in my womb, overflowing at night, simultaneously bringing me towards and pushing me further away from my mother.

'How am I going to clean that?' I thought in a panic. Not exactly thought, but that which precedes thought. A foreboding, taking fright, a malaise. Her, standing next to me, looking down on me, waiting to see what I will do. Will I remove the sheet and leave it to soak all night in the bath? Take a flannel, wet it with cold water and rub the stain on the mattress until it is practically invisible? Until I can do no more, exhausted by the labour and my self-hatred? She would never have made the bed without an undersheet. She couldn't bear stains on the mattress, betraying intimacy. She taught me to pre-empt the marks left by the body, its impurities. To always expect the worst. To fight blood like an enemy.

We were on holiday at the time. Despite the double thickness of blanket, the blood, a dark, irregular trickle, had penetrated the brocade covering the double bed. Filtered by the layers of protection it had only made a tiny stain, just a drop. I hoped she would not see it.

'I saw,' she told me that afternoon in the garden. The harshness of her voice seemed to make the long grass tremble behind me. I went back into the house and filled a glass of water; her words seemed to have dried my lips. I stood there, glass in hand, breathing deeply: suddenly the air smelt of sulphur.

I knew what she meant: she was aware of my secret, understood that I had tried to hide it.

I turned round.

Her eyes, light velvet brown in daylight, were almost black. Again I heard the rustle of the grass, like someone fleeing as our eyes met. I looked down at my stomach, still wet from my swim. There were white traces of salt. I wiped them away with my palm which was suddenly damp.

'I will kill myself or go mad if you do that again, if you stain the mattress,' she said quietly, as if to herself.

It wasn't an accusation or a threat. It was a statement, as if spots of blood could really make her lose her reason. In the garden, before my eyes, a crack had appeared on her face. A narrow diagonal line, scarcely visible, destroying the harmony. She looked straight past me at an unavoidable danger of which I was still unaware, a harbinger of death that she alone could recognise. My blood was just its external sign, but, at that moment, in her eyes, it assumed the power of a symbol.

'I didn't do it on purpose,' I finally contended, hoping the sound of my voice would bring her to her senses.

She looked at me as if I was part of a world to which she had no access.

When I entered my bedroom later I found a rubber undersheet folded on the bed. I put it in the wardrobe. That evening it was there again – a white square in the gloom. My mother had come in and lifted up the bedclothes to make sure that I had used it. Seeing I hadn't obeyed her she snatched it out of the wardrobe and threw it down on the bed. Furious, frightened. Her eyes still glowed like black coals.

She had the strength to do that, to make these gestures against me.

She thought that mine was a hopeless case, that nothing could be done with me. It was no longer just the brocade covering the double bed, but a rite of passage: I now belonged to another category of women, those who leave behind them traces of their nauseating femininity. What could she expect of me, if not betrayal? She believed, no doubt, that it was too late now, that she would be powerless from then on: I would soon be intoxicated by my own body. She found it hard to cope with the presence of my blood in the house. It was perhaps then that she repudiated me, me, that girl who was incapable of understanding that femininity is a dangerous burden.

I follow that wet patch back through time – impossible to do otherwise. This has happened before! This has happened before! Disgust, fear. I recognise the moment of divorce from my own body (can the crack yawning inside my mother also exist in me?) I push it away in order to take care of it like a sick dependant. As she taught me to do.

I thought this sensation would never be repeated. But there, lying on my side, curled up beneath the old cherry-red bedspread, I am no longer sure of anything. Neither of the time in which I am living nor of my age. And she pushes me into the abyss behind me, lets me fall, does nothing to hold me back.

I fall, deeper and deeper. I see myself fall, endlessly.

I am twelve years old. The towel gripped between my thighs is already soaked and I know that if I do not act blood will flow onto my nightdress then onto the sheet, the mattress, the floor – further, into the corridor, into her room. I feel I am losing enormous quantities, that my blood will soon flood the whole house, that we will drown, both of us, in the thick, dark red liquid. It all started quite recently and I'm not yet used to the rites and customs of the adult world. I don't dare wake her up. I stand in the dark as the trickle runs down my thighs. I go to the bathroom. The water is so cold my teeth chatter. I am afraid that she will hear this unwelcome noise and come and find me crouching in the bath, naked, transfixed . . . I do not dry myself on a towel for fear of dirtying it. I take off my nightdress, roll it into a ball and wedge it between my legs. I go back to bed taking care to avoid the wet patch.

She wakes me at dawn.

'You have sullied everything,' she says.

She uses this strange, uncommon, almost obsolete word in order to choke back the swear word already on the tip of her tongue.

'Get out and clean that lot up.'

I sit in the bed, naked, and cry. My guilt overflows; I feel I will never free myself of it. The nightdress screwed up between my legs has a pattern of yellow sunflowers.

The body, like a curse.

It started with the smell of lime-trees in blossom. I was at the open-air cinema when, for the first time, I felt the sly pain in my abdomen, a prickling – like yesterday evening. A malaise melding with the sweet, intoxicating fragrance of the lime-trees. I went home alone with a small wet patch on the back of my dress, betraying me. I see again my narrow back, my copper hair cascading wildly about my shoulders, the wide silk ribbon round my waist . . . Still today nausea grips me every time I visualise the ends of the ribbon floating on the evening breeze, the sky-blue organdie dress with the stain behind, right in the middle, a first trace of blood.

I only realised afterwards. I did not yet know what it meant. I walked slowly down the road looking in shop windows with this accusing mark behind me.

In the bathroom the first thing she said was: 'You have to wash blood quickly in cold water, otherwise it leaves a stain.' She snatched my little knickers from the edge of the bath, filled the sink and put them in to soak. They were white with small red spots. The water went pink, as if colour was running from the spots. She scrubbed them vigorously then put them in a bowl with hot water and washing powder. Lumps of undissolved powder swam to the surface. She crushed them between her fingers, lost in thought.

Image: her hands diving into the pink water and fishing out the spotty knickers, tiny knickers, a child's knickers still. She holds them in front of her for a moment, surprised – as if what has happened is absolutely unexpected, incredible.

She also seems to have the impression that colour is running from the red spots.

When she looked down at me, then, I felt her hesitate between tenderness and firmness. I could almost touch the cleft in her thoughts. I saw that she had something to say to me. But she did not dare for fear of wounding me and making me bleed even more.

She gave it up.

In an undecided, flat voice, a shadowy voice inhabited, I felt, by some ghost, she murmured that it happened to women every month and that I would recognise the start by the pain in my abdomen.

She doubtless saw my hands clutching the edge of the washbasin when she said 'women'.

I am not sure she saw it. She pushed the bowl under the great old bath, into the dark, between the cast iron feet shaped like lions' paws. One day when I dropped something – a hair grip, some soap – the bowl was sticking out a little. I drew it towards me. Floating in the red water, like in a great open wound, was her bloodstained underwear. Pink foam clung round the edge.

Blood, secret.

Blood, a blow of the fist.

I remember that the bathroom was full of some unknown smell, bitter, diluted blood and linen that has soaked for too long, lavender soap, my fear. Abruptly she pushed the bowl back under the bath: a little water splashed on the floor. She wiped it up straight away: no, no, it's nothing, it doesn't exist, this world that smells of decomposition.

Forget it. Don't forget it.

'Lock the door,' she said.

This command had a different ring now: a precise meaning, coloured red, and its own smell. Her words hung in the air, defining that specific space, under the bath, damp, shadow, blindness, silence. Silence. Things you don't talk about but which enchain you all the same.

Carefully, with her fingertips, she stripped off my organdie dress – I would never again wear it as the stain never came out, even after she boiled it. She grabbed my arm, frightened I would dart away, that I would escape.

'Come here so I can wash you.'

Even though for years I had been washing myself, I offered no resistance. I crouched in the bath. She grabbed the shower and began by spraying the tepid water on my face. She let it run for a while, flowing gently down my features, in my mouth, along my neck . . . If I'd cried she wouldn't have known. Then she took the round soap from the edge of the bath, a child's soap, and washed me. Between my knees, in the gloom where I buried my head, I saw the blood falling drop by drop onto the floor of the bath; running away with the water. It relieved me.

Now her open palms slide along my neck, my shoulders, my arms, my back. She is thinking that this is the last time, that I would never let her do it again. Her hands slide tenderly down the spine, over the hips.

The little one needs washing, today, she needs it. Gently. One part of her body then another. With this child's soap I've been using ever since she was born. Then abandon her to her destiny. It's finished, finished. She will swim with the current, like a little boat. Already, irredeemably, she escapes me. Everything says so: her soft, diaphanous flesh; her thick, burnished red hair; her bowed, slightly-protruding upper lip. As if she already knows what it is to kiss. Her delicate joints, her long neck. The way she sits down, leaning on the chair back and looking round the room. She looks. She touches. With her eyes, like with fingers, she explores the faces. People smile, uncomfortably, at this child with prematurely old eyes.

In the bathroom she gazes at the hips which will soon widen, the still unformed breasts – all that which has yet to surface. Now she is inside me, under my skin. She probes me, recognising me as another her – a small female animal who will grow up, who will suffer. She foresees the knocks awaiting me. Men's hands on me.

'I can do nothing for her,' she thinks. 'What a sad day.'

I have never forgotten the sadness of that day, as she washed me her hands on my shoulders became heavier and heavier.

Nothing can erase my obsession with cleanliness. I get up, remove the sheet and put it in the bath. I turn on the tap. I run the water. I scrub the stain which pales. Cold water removes bloodstains, just as she told me. I pour in soap powder and with her gestures – with her hands – I crush the white, twenty-year-old lumps. It's all useless, I could just as well have used the washing machine. But in her house bloodstains must be washed by hand.

It's a penitence, as if she's reproaching me, still punishing me today. If I don't wash out this stain by hand, as she taught me, if I don't obey her voice echoing inside me, I will never come close to her. I will lose her. I will lose her while I still need her, her love that is still fear. Half asleep I wonder if, despite myself, I make these same gestures at home, if I launch myself into this vigorous, futile prewash, signifying a repressed desire of the body to destroy those traces, to destroy them. Have I lived all this time unaware? I thought I had freed myself of the need to imitate her, safe in my minuscule bathroom crammed with dirty washing overflowing the washing basket and piling up in corners, drip-drying on a string over the bath, draped over the radiators. In her bathroom I suddenly realise there is a certain order governing mine – a long-established order, in the way I don't hang or fold things up, I iron things all anyhow. It has done me no good, it seems, to leave, to journey, to force myself to forget. Actions looming up out of the abysses of primordial life have conquered me, erasing the trouble I have taken, time and myself.

She is in the kitchen. Ironing. On a chair next to her she piles the starched and dampened washing. First she takes a sheet. She folds it in half, taking care to match the edges. Then the iron, with large expansive gestures. On the sheet wide, depthless furrows are formed. She folds it again, smooths out the hems. Stiffened by starch, the sheets squeak as she piles them up on the end of the table: one, two, three, four. Four white cotton sheets, four pillow cases, clean linen for her bed and for mine. Flattening creases, destroying dirt, the iron purifies them of all trace of the night.

The knickers come last – they are buried at the bottom of the pile under the bath towels and napkins, the tablecloths, T-shirts and dishcloths. They too are made of white cotton. 'So they can be boiled,' she says. 'White, one hundred per cent cotton, that you can boil.' To iron them, first of all she turns them over. Then she stretches the elastic and slides the iron across. Sometimes the violence of her actions surprises me: she presses down with all her strength, several times, on the narrow, lined gusset.

The damp material gives off a corrosive smell of bleach.

When she rinses them after boiling them, she puts a little greenish liquid in the clear water. To make them even whiter. There is a skull on the bottle with a cross through it. For a while the odour of poison hangs on the air in the bathroom.

For me it is the odour of cleanliness. A comforting smell, immaculate.

I am cold, I am dark. I am standing in the middle of the bathroom with the light on – a big white lamp up there on the ceiling. So what. Something has happened: I have the clear sensation that time is flowing through me like a hollow carcass, a hole in space, that it is dragging me towards a place where I can no longer imagine or control it. I am frightened. Very frightened. Nothing can protect me from this force flowing against the current.

I notice the walls have been newly tiled. I have never seen them before. They look like they have been soaked one at a time in a bath full of water made pink by blood then stuck back on the wall. The surface is still wet – pink and viscous like the damp mucous membrane of the uterus. The watery blood oozing from it makes me nauseous.

Place of hate. Place of love.

I approach the mirror but I already know that I won't see myself in it. Her toiletries, laid out on the shelf, invite transformation: a few empty bottles of foundation, cold cream, three bars of soap, still wrapped, a round, silver face-powder, a black eye-pencil, a deodorant.

Her otherness.

All that is her. Each one of those objects. So many traps laid for my senses, a prison to lose me in, flesh into which I melt . . .

I see her standing in front of the mirror. She is examining herself. Lifts her arm well above her head to see her armpit. In the mirror I clearly see her profile and the exposed armpit. She takes the deodorant. The wet ball slides across her skin from top to bottom. From top to bottom. From top to bottom. She breathes the fragrance. I smell it too, an odour of irises instantly evaporating on contact with her warm skin.

I hesitate between the need to gaze over and again at her reflection, her gestures, and the desire to flee this dangerous place where I am dissolving. The words do not exist to express my love for her, no words, they have not yet been invented. Words refer to other things, a relationship which goes without saying. They reject this love-passion. But it is here, in me. Bodily. Present. In the odour of her armpit. Love – feverish, exclusive, unique, blinding – like hate.

In the bathroom there are no tampons, not even any napkins – just cotton wool. I put a great wad between my legs to be sure of having enough. When, back in my room, I look for a pair of knickers in my case I realise that all the ones I have brought are cotton, 'one hundred per cent cotton, that you can boil'. I can no longer escape the images emanating from the clothes, the furniture, the smell of lavender and wax, the window frame, the initials embroidered on the sheet, the round handles on the wardrobe doors, my own fingers suddenly burning me, as if licked by flames.

The openings onto the outside world are closed. I know that I will not leave here until the past has been completely drained out of me, like a torrent.

Until the house has vomited it out.

To forget. To no longer remember, to instantly lose memory.

To sink in self-forgetfulness as in healing sleep.

It's too late.

2

It must have been about seven o'clock when I arrived yesterday evening. The sun had already set and the shadow of the house was melting into the tarry darkness. Now it's night, some unknown hour of the night. In this house the timepieces and the alarm clocks do not work – if they did, time would be seen to flow backwards. In the opaque night I press my forehead to the windowpane and, for a moment, feel that I am touching the black vortex deep inside me, deep inside where living images wrench themselves whole from my muscles, my stomach, my palate, from inside my eyeballs from the tips of my fingers.

A beautiful woman. They said of her that she was a beautiful woman.

Her beauty was exclusive. Her presence put those around her in the shade, made them transparent. Close to her, they suddenly became small, wrinkled, black, dirty – second-class beings. Her beauty was stupefying, violent, emptying the space around her. I don't know if she realised that she destroyed her surroundings. She walked with her head held high and seemed to see nothing. Her legs and her hips moved as one, bewitchingly supple. People would turn to look at her like a doll, to see what she was made of. I well knew how men would wheel about her like hawks at first astonished and afraid, then lustful. In their eyes I could sometimes see an unknown hunger, not of the body but of the purity of forms. Later I discovered the same expression in the gaze of art lovers. A particular focussed gaze that reveals beauty.

We were at the municipal beach. They sat down, her and her friend, on the jetty, right by the sea. The woman, wearing a one-piece swimsuit, was lying on her stomach. When she moved a dark red mark appeared all across her back. I examined this white, fleshy back, the place where the circulation was cut off by the too-tight swimsuit, the line of her hips, her legs carelessly parted, her toes pressed against the concrete slab . . . My mother was next to her. All at once I was convinced that there was an obvious and irredeemable difference between them, and looked about me. The sun had already sunk down into the sea and the beach was almost deserted. A group of men passed by: their glances floated on my mother like oil on water. It might have been the soft light of the setting sun or the way she threw her head back when she smiled, but she was beautiful. Unmistakable.

Perhaps it was the warm dusk, perhaps the way the rays of the distant sun struck her as I watched, something made me partially capture the meaning of the word 'beauty': in the line of her raised leg, one crossed over the other; in this peaceful, confident body; in the lightness with which she gave herself to the caress of the sunset, to the gaze of passers by. Each of her gestures radiated a harmony of which she was unaware. She had let down her hair. She leaned back a little and her hair spread out in waves over her shoulders. From where I was sitting I could only *see*, this gesture but I also *heard* the murmur of her long, dark, dishevelled hair, the sound of it on the skin of her shoulders. There, close up against my ear.

As if I was her, again.

Her friend lay alongside, in shadow, dark, hard. Her movements stiff. There was something unfinished about her.

I felt that she too had become aware of something which made her uncomfortable. She pulled the end of her bath towel towards her and covered herself. When she stood up I saw the marks made by the little regular squares of concrete on her thighs: a mesh of imperfection.

Impossible to hide them.

With her innocent cruelty my mother said:

'Stay a bit longer, while there's still some sun.'

'I'm going in,' said the woman. 'It's getting cold.'

She felt the reflection of my mother's beauty insinuating itself under her skin, her body becoming alien, escaping her. She was ashamed. Lost in thought she ran her fingers over the thick, horny skin of her heels, her poorly-shaved legs, the flaccid insides of her thighs. She thought that her skin hung like rags, scarcely attached to her skeleton at all.

I hate her, she said to herself, as if my mother's presence corroded her, like acid.

When she had gone my mother became pale. For a moment she gazed motionless at the sea, thoughtful, abandoned to her beauty, imprisoned in it like a shell. Then she stood up: on her pinched face and lips I saw an expression of cold determination, of a rift in her relationship with the world; the line that she should not cross, at the risk of leaving herself, appeared, plainly visible.

I have known it too, this turning in on oneself, this assault, this poison – this unbearable daily presence separating me from my body. My mother seemed closer to me than my own body and I felt I had to pass through her in order to reach myself.

I felt she was too close.

The previous evening we had seen an Ava Gardner film. In one scene she leant forward and we could see the marks left by her swimsuit's shoulder straps because of the weight of her breasts. I was sitting in the middle of the canoe, leaning slightly forward. How thin her back is, my mother must have thought, how bad her posture is. She wanted to grasp my shoulders and straighten me out. But beneath her fingers she felt the mark, like in the film. The shoulder straps of my swimsuit cutting into my flesh.

She looked at me. Looked at my breasts. It's their weight which makes her stoop, she said to herself. When did that happen? When? How could her bosom have developed like that without me notic- ing, surging out of nowhere in one night, burgeon- ing from this thin, still-unformed body?

Her hand stops, hesitates. Pulls back from my shoulders as if I disgusted her or as if she had been caught doing something prohibited – touching an alien, unknown skin. She ought to remember, though, I thought. She ought to remember that she has already seen them, and recently.

I was walking down the street. Some workmen were digging a trench. One of them leaned his two hands with their black fingernails on the handle of his shovel. He watched me. No, not me, my breasts. For the first time I felt clearly that they existed. They became suddenly remote, distanced by his stare. I felt they were both alien and unbearably heavy. I had to pass close by him, crossing the trench on a plank. He said: 'Buy yourself a bra.' I ran, ran home. I had to hold my breasts with my hands to stop the pain. How come she didn't see my breasts when I got in? My breasts – which didn't belong to me – clinging to the sweat-soaked T-shirt. How come she didn't see how out of breath I was, how disturbed I was, my desire to tell her everything. I expected her to see it. Her eye rested upon me for a moment, but all I saw in it was the tiny white reflection of my T-shirt. Nothing more.

Now, at last, she sees them.

Her eye hesitates still, refusing to accept what she sees, putting off till later, always later, the need to admit. Her fingertips still recall their contact with my skin, the mark. Like a blind person, only touch could allow her this startling awareness, communicated from her fingers to her brain: I am a woman.

Her fingers losing themselves in my femininity.

56

She felt the saliva collect in her mouth and, suddenly losing her beautiful poise, thought that the undeniable presence of my body was going to make her vomit.

She grasped the edge of the canoe.

At that moment, I know, she felt the weight of her own breasts stretching her bra.

She recalled the way she removed it in the half-darkness of the bedroom. My father awaits this moment. He turns on the bedside lamp to illuminate the patch of naked, milk-white flesh, alone of all her tanned body. With his fingers he follows the delicate tracery of veins just below the skin as if it was a map that he was trying to memorise. Then he grasps the breasts in his hands, like apples, feeling their weight. He doesn't raise his eyes. How strange that he hasn't yet looked at me, she thinks, feeling a sly pain in her chest.

He lowers himself to sit down next to her. Kisses her neck and shoulder first, very gently, just brushing them with his lips. Then, timidly, he leans towards the nipple.

She feels the milk come.

He lowers himself further. Now he is kneeling in front of her, as if praying. Eyes closed, he presses his lips first to one nipple, then to the other. He doesn't suck, just strokes them with the end of his tongue. But the milk flows of its own accord, running down onto my mother's belly.

'It's sweet,' he murmurs, almost inaudibly.

'Stop,' she murmurs, not moving, holding firmly, her hands around his head. Greedily he licks the milk from her body and lays his wet face against her stomach.

At this moment she is fully aware of her power.

In the canoe it is hot. Her hands still grip the wooden rail, she gazes at her unsteady reflection in the sea. The brightness of the sun makes her head ache. She looks for her sunglasses. It is only when she has put them on that she feels strong enough to look at him. He is sitting in the prow of the little boat, smoking, the tall stranger who is taking us for a boat ride. Her eyes question: could he have seen the same thing as her? But he is looking at the waves, the white hem of the coast in the distance. As if he hadn't noticed her hand on my shoulder, her hesitation, her malaise, her faintness and then her long abstraction. Her fear.

Now she looks at me. She imagines me taking off my bra in front of this man, approaching him, closer and closer, melting under his gaze. I read all that in her features, in her face that perfection is abandoning: her lips tremble, as if she is going to cry at the mere thought that such a thing could occur. Then, very quickly, she chases the fearful image from her mind and becomes confident again.

No, no, no, he saw nothing, she thinks. Nothing. Not yet.

She's only a child, she's only a child, she repeats to herself and that comforts her.

The man is sitting in the prow of the canoe, smoking. Inscrutable, he puffs out wisps of smoke and gazes at the sea. He saw everything; well before her, well before me. Now his eyes do not even glance at us: they could betray him. In his gaze we are identical, two women's bodies in swimsuits.

They look so alike, he thinks, same breasts, same face, same lips, same hair . . . Like two sisters.

'Anyone would think you were sisters,' someone said, looking at a photograph.

We were sitting together on the steps of a church. I had a narrow, serious expression and wild hair like hers. She smiled when she heard this. Oh, how I wanted to hug her then! I would so have wished her not to be my mother, to cut the cord that ties me to her, to spit out once and for all the bitterness she smears on my throat each day.

She would talk to me of men. Would show me her silk underwear. We would laugh together. From our room would burst uncontrollable giggles, gurgles and hiccups that we would try to stifle by putting our hands over our mouths. I would never betray her, never search through her drawers and her wardrobes, looking for proof of the duplicity that I vaguely foresee in her. I would not want to penetrate to the heart of her, into the soft flesh, to emerge at the other end liberated from the thick, opaque mucous membranes in which she wraps me.

I have no sister. I have only her. And she remains silent.

To learn to know her I had to become her. It was the only way of breaking through her silence. She had no voice but objects betrayed her because they spoke her language – the language of the body. I had to get into her bed, her wardrobes, put on her dresses and shoes, wash with her perfumed soaps, do my hair with her combs. I rummaged in her dressing table drawers, in the bathroom, in the chest of drawers, in her old handbags. That's how I learnt that there is not only cotton wool and glycerine soap, but also silk and body lotions. I knew everything about her garters, her corsets, her figure-hugging evening gowns slit to the hip. About her shoes with old-fashioned heels. About the sheaf of carefully-tied letters in German. About the pictures used for marking pages in the prayer books that she secreted round the house.

In the bedside table was a flat silver packet containing a black, see-through nightdress. I removed it and spread it out on the bed: it was long and low cut with a double flounce around the bottom. At first I thought it looked like my coffee-coloured crêpe-de-Chine summer dress, the flounced one with the pleats beneath the bosom.

I put it on.

Why the long sleeves? I wondered, as if had that nightdress had short sleeves it would have been less painful for me to discover that there were men for whom she put it on. In order to appear naked before them.

That's how he sees her – how he sees her body as she moves about the middle of the bedroom, for him.

There was something unhealthy, unbearable, in the way I examined this garment, at the same time her and myself, but with the eyes of a third person. The moment I put it on I felt a shock, as though I had touched an electric cable. I no longer knew who I was, I was incapable of knowing. I felt that someone was watching me through the transparent material. I feel his mysterious presence still haunting the bedroom today. Under the double gaze reflected by the mirror the nightdress clung to my skin like a fine membrane, a film of wax.

On the bedside table I saw the nail scissors.

Something welled up inside me, without me being aware of it. Slowly, like in a ballet, I stretched out an arm sheathed with transparent silk towards the scissors. The next moment I saw my tense, feverish hand lacerate the nightdress. Slowly, laboriously, the blade advanced, leaving behind an irregular round void. I felt powerless, overcome by the effort necessary to continue what I had begun – the impulse that had made me grasp the ridiculously small scissors had suddenly disappeared.

Finish this dissection, it must be finished.

Perhaps she has never worn it, I mused. The thought floated for a moment on the air, bright and sumptuous like hope. But it was too late. My diaphragm rose and shuddered, uprooting something like sobs from my insides. Hesitant, they paused for a moment in my lungs before bursting to the surface.

I folded the nightdress up again and returned it to its box. I had discovered her secret: the presence of a third person. I knew she would never forgive me but there was no way back. When I had put the silver packet back in place I thought: There's nothing she can do to me. I felt I had rid myself of a dangerous illness, a fatal illness.

The silence that weighs on the house and on our lacerated, separated lives still binds us.

She taught me the language of silence – the meaning of gestures, murmurs and perfumes, strangled cries and unfinished phrases. She taught me to recognise the substructure of words, movements in the darkness, eyes that suddenly turn away, treacherous silence.

I think it was an abortion, though she never uttered the word. In her mouth it would have taken on a metallic ring, like a poorly-understood foreign language spoken out loud for the first time.

'She's lost a lot of blood.'

In the peaceful apartment among the quiet footfalls I heard this phrase spoken half aloud. It wasn't addressed to me. My mother lay on the living room sofa. She was not alone. Through the half-open door I could hear whispers punctuated by silence. There was someone near her, a man; from time to time he obscured from me her closed eyes and extraordinarily small, bloodless, unmade-up mouth. He got up and took a few anxious steps about the room before pushing his chair nearer to the sofa. I could clearly see his profile, his aquiline nose and his slightly receding chin. I saw him slowly stroke her forehead with his thin hand; he stroked her gently, absently, as one strokes a sick child. He leaned forward and whispered something. She did not open her eyes, did not move. I was sure that she was in pain, terrible pain. Calm, pale, wrapped in silence and the sweetish odour of decomposition, she was on the point of death: this man leaning towards her no doubt brought comfort to her last moments. He wore a sort of uniform, a navy blue jacket of stiff cloth with gold epaulettes. The gilding and the slow caress made a solemn, sad impression, like in church.

Blood, blood flowing out of my mother in torrents, exhausting her, bringing this blue tinge, indistinct.

I know that the sheets beneath her are wet with red, that the velvet sofa cover is absorbing the thick liquid wrenching itself from her guts in dark clots. Then it becomes lighter, thinner. Her body shrinks; suddenly the man shudders and takes his hand away from her forehead: my mother's head has become absolutely flat. I watch through the half-open door, my heart pounding – the hall walls send the insidious echo of its beating ricocheting back towards me.

To die instead of her; the viscous red evil would flow suddenly out of me.

When the man with the epaulettes had left she called me.

'Sit down near me,' she said.

Her voice was not quite extinguished; she was still capable of giving orders. I sat down where he had been sitting – the chair retained the impression left by his heavy body.

'I will soon recover, you know . . .'

The 'you know', superfluous and uncertain, spoken as if she expected some help from me that was essential to her getting better. Her body exuded a damp sickly heat that rose in waves towards my face. She looked at me, imploring me to give some sign, some aid, some confrontation. Understanding perhaps. Yes, I ought to understand her and accept everything without a word – her, the smell of blood, the gold epaulettes, the pain, her powerlessness, everything. Without a word.

She breathed slowly and irregularly like a weak animal. She took a box of chocolates from the table.

'Have one.'

The dumb weight that pinned her to the floor, this rending, unexpressed pain, finally she pushed them towards me with all her strength: the box of chocolates in neat, decorative twists of paper was now between us, like a mass of words waiting to be spoken. It filled the space separating our bodies in which our breaths mingled.

I understood. The sweets must be eaten, unwrapped and sucked, melted in the mouth. They tasted of the words flooding her mouth but which she would never speak.

She stroked my hair with her eyes closed. Her restrained touch could be interpreted any number of ways: an explanation, a justification, simultaneously

a kind of admission of responsibility and a submission.

'What beautiful hair you have,' she said.

This is the only caress I can remember. Now and
then she would run her fingers through my long red
hair like this and seemed to take pleasure in trying to
untangle it with her fingers. It would last a long time,
separating the ruffled tresses, then she would brush
them with a wooden-handled bristle hairbrush.

'It still does least damage to the hair,' she would
say, as if addressing the plait she was making. 'Does
that hurt?'

'No, no,' I would reply, fuddled by the touch of
her hands.

Feeling her so close almost made my head spin.
She would stand behind me, gently leaning her
stomach and her breasts against my back. I felt her
through my dress, burning me and making my flesh
melt. I sucked her in. Hungrily I swallowed her
body through this searing wound in my back.

Her hands rummaged through my hair, separating the locks and pulling them backwards. My
hair obeyed, slipping through her fingers, awkward
and submissive at the same time.

Now she is in front of me. I do not raise my head:
I watch the vein pulsing in her neck, just under the
skin – the place where her weakness and vulner-
ability show through that I alone can see. Alone.

Desire to plant my lips there and feel her pulse with my tongue.

It only lasts a moment – a flash of madness, of love – then finally I raise my eyes to her face.

Against the headrest of the sofa it looks different, surrounded by her loose hair. Softer, lighter, rounder. A shadow transforms it, softening the pure, severe line of her forehead, her prominent cheekbones. She rarely undoes the bun of hair in the nape of her neck, freeing her mane of locks that cascade halfway down her back. She washes her hair on her own, as if this is her most important way of getting in touch with herself. Her wet hair is at first smooth, a dripping black mass. Then the fine, curly tresses reform, shining with the dark blue of the night sky. In the air her hair dries quickly. As she passes by an odour of camomile shampoo, vinegar water for rinsing her hair and clean, cool skin – what I called 'her smell'. Sometimes, when I entered her bedroom, it invaded my nostrils.

I felt like I was close to her then, breathing pressed up against her eyelids: heavy odour, sweet, dense, dark . . . I know now that it was the smell of her hair.

Already, as she passed her fingers through mine, as she pronounced the word 'beautiful', I knew that I would get it cut. Her caress was that of a weakened, exhausted, crushed woman. It seemed to follow the invisible line that linked me to her, her hair and mine, abortion and death. I felt this steel rope tighten around me as I leant over her.

I never used to go to the hairdresser's. She cut off my split ends for me. Now, in the hair salon window, a photograph of a young woman with short hair, leaning on a mauve curtain. Pouting, the girl gazes at the park on the other side of the road.

That's what I want to look like, I said to myself and went in. The salon was empty.

'I want a haircut like that,' I told the stylist, pointing to the photograph in the window.

My voice seemed hesitant, as if my mother might at any moment call into question the words it uttered.

The stylist was doing her nails. The noise of the nail file and the dry dust on her fingertips made me shiver. She put the nail file down on the counter and I saw her name, Victoria, engraved in black letters on its white plastic handle. It reassured me. I took a seat and relaxed.

The first snip of the scissors and I knew I was betraying mother.

I would tell her that my hair annoyed me, that it made me too hot . . . I would invent an excuse, anything. I had to. I couldn't admit to her that I no longer wanted to carry the burden of our similitude and that this was the only way of telling her.

To cut the bonds, the bonds which link hair, blood and decomposition.

The stylist took off my pigtail in one stroke.

'Would you like me to wrap it up? Do you want to keep it as a souvenir?'

Go home. With her watching, open my hands full of cut hair. It slips silently to the floor.

'Yes, yes, please,' I said, timidly, as if frightened of changing my mind.

She tied the pigtail at each end with white elastic bands and laid it on a piece of paper, like a long, lifeless copper snake. When I picked it up, I was amazed at how heavy it was.

In the mirror I saw an oblong face gazing back at me, with great big eyes which seemed lighter without the crown of hair. The scissors seemed to have erased the shadows of insecurity and doubt which darkened them. It could have been a boy's face. Yes, that was definitely what I looked like from a distance – a boy, still shooting up. Relieved, I winked at my new image and imitated the expression of the girl in the window. When I went out into the street I felt the caress of the sun on my uncluttered cheeks.

When she saw me she froze. Then she started towards her bedroom, as if she needed time to take in this abrupt change, to reflect in peace. I sat down on the threshold of the balcony, my head leaning

on a pane of glass. I held an open book on my
knees – I still remember the texture of the pages
and the leather cover embossed with gold letters. I
knew she was going to come back and say something to me.

I waited.

Still in the doorway of her room she saw me, head
thrown back, the book on my knees. My fingers
explored the book's cover, abstractedly. Suddenly
my neck seemed too long to her – or, rather, it
seemed alien. Her questioning gaze slipped down
my profile and, just for a moment, I thought I saw
her hesitate: she didn't recognise me. The image of
me in her head no longer coincided with the one
reflected in her eyes.

It was only then that she saw that I had had my
hair cut, that my new boyish style uncluttered
my face, brought out my pale eyes, the arc of my
eyebrows, the line of my nose and my full lips,
inviting, making my face confident, insolent, chal-
lenging. You can see everything now, she thought,
as if my hair had been hiding the hard nut of my
sexuality.

I remembered the film *Bonjour Tristesse*, the scene
where Jean Seberg is in bed with the sheet pulled
up under her chin. I recalled her seductive, naked
face.

Seduction of the naked face.

70

It was exposed, now, to men's eyes. They could examine freely the shell of my ears, the dark place behind and the hollow in the nape of my neck, the dip beside my collarbone which fills with water in the bath. For the first time she was aware of how alike we looked and saw that from now on people would see it. Nevertheless, she should have seen something else: that I wanted to change, that I was retreating, that, unconsciously, I was trying to escape her piercing, questioning gaze, her suspicion, that I didn't deserve yet.

She left her bedroom and came and stood next to me. Pushed her fingers through my now nonexistent hair.

'Stupid girl,' she said, 'you stupid little girl.'

It was as if she was saying 'What's the use? That changes nothing. You don't know yourself why you did it. You are incapable of knowing. Incapable.'

There was already a third person between us, an invisible man who looked at me with her eyes.

Me too, I saw this man with my mother's eyes.

It's New Year's Eve. She puts on her navy blue dress; the cold silk slips down over her hips. This delicate, clinging low-cut dress. I notice it when, before leaving, she leans over to make sure that the seam on her stockings is straight: she straightens the black line on her calf then runs her finger all the way up her leg. It runs higher and higher. It is so quiet that I can hear the tiny crackle of the nail catching on the nylon. The finger stops on the thigh, just above the dark hem.

Her flesh where the stocking ends.

Her flesh in her cleavage.

It feels like her breasts are resting in my hands as she leans over, half naked, her leg stretched out behind her. Like a porcelain ballerina, like a petrified statue, completely engrossed in herself. At this moment she is conscious of the desire that will be aroused by the diaphanous skin above the hem of her stocking, by her deep, dark cleavage, by her hands in their white kid, elbow-length gloves and the clinging silk flattering her figure and the curve of her hips. She stands there, immobile, frozen in mid-gesture, full of the promise of what may happen . . . of what will definitely happen this night.

Then she comes back to life and leaves. She walks head high as if she has just taken some weighty decision that only she knows about. When she has closed the door I will remember the furtive kiss she gave my cheek on leaving me, the way I touched it with my hand and the sweet, penetrating smell left in my palm.

In a black and white photograph taken during that New Year's Eve party she is smiling, standing on the left. Near her, four other people, three men and one woman. Glass in hand, she leans her shoulder lightly against that of a man with a strong, wilful jaw and brushed back wavy hair; there is a little confetti clinging to the lapel of his jacket. Slightly constrained they raise their glasses to the person holding the camera.

But the photograph's centre of gravity is her.

The eye does not rest on the four unknown smiling figures, it dips down to her cleavage, inundating the horizon. It seems here that at any moment the silk will melt and reveal further this white skin emerging from her bodice with every breath. But three silver and glass buttons are there to stop the flesh from spreading, arresting the eye where the cloth ends, where the promise begins, brushing against the sense of anticipation floating between her and the man, born out of the light touch of her shoulder against his, as if marking out her territory. There, on the sleeve of his woollen blazer, you feel tension.

A little later she will go to him. She will blow on the confetti stuck to his lapel and make them fall, then she will slide her hands between the jacket and the shirt. Her fingers feel the smooth, straight back. He is troubled at first by her daring, no doubt. Then his lips seek to cut a path to her bosom beneath the blue silk bodice. The whiteness of this falsely-virginal skin excites him and, with his teeth – as if robbed of the use of his hands or as if he no longer wanted to wrench them from his sides – he tears off the three shiny buttons and undresses her, at last. As the dress slips slowly to the floor she has the impression, in this unknown bedroom, that the wind is creeping in through the opening of the window and stirring up eddies of silver flecks. But she soon realises that it is just a ray of light, a ray of watery light, winter moonlight no doubt.

As a moon knife, she thinks, shutting her eyes, already in the bed, already giving in to the heat radiating from her groin beneath the man's impetuous caress.

While they lie naked, stuck together, she opens her eyes for a brief moment and notices that the first rays of dawn are already squeezing through the curtain. The blond hairs on her arm stand up; uncertainty has already slipped in between her and the man in her arms: memory of the silver knife which separates bodies. The image throbs and she cannot put it out of her mind.

She looks at him, a guilty smile on her lips.

She shuts her eyes again. If she wakes up completely she will clearly see, in the grey light of dawn, the face of the stranger lying next to her. She will have the impression – no, she will know for sure – that none of that concerns her, that she is already elsewhere. That she is no longer in this bed, in these arms, suddenly demanding and brutal. More and more distant she will see him, down there, lying next to her peaceful, uncovered body which suddenly relaxes and sinks in absence, in death.

He will not notice her expression, nor the chasm yawning between them.

Safety of closed eyes: the heavy man's body becomes light again, so light – almost nonexistent. Outside herself, all the same she delights in her ability to make these deep, staccato sighs burst from him like sobs. She takes pleasure in seeing him watching her, through nearly-closed eyelids, bewitched, burning, damp, sick . . . contaminated by a germ of pleasure in which he is losing himself.

She hates him. She hates this moment of complete abandon, when his movements become abrupt and violent, just before they end in an echoless spasm.

But she says: 'Again!'

Again, again – until he is empty, capable of seeing through her game perhaps.

In the morning she feels dirty. Filth has collected in her mouth. Still half asleep, she recognises the bitterness tightening her throat and threatening to overflow from the corner, dribbling onto the pillow, wet, sickening trace of one more night.

It's always the same, she thinks, drowsily.

Then she slowly swallows the sour phlegm, the dry, plastery deposit clinging to her palate that she can neither spit out nor rinse. She knows that this is her punishment. She remembers the night past, recognises the price that must be paid and the mucus slips more easily down her dry throat.

That summer, her pleasure must have come without warning. She was beginning to get old and expected nothing more. She knew now how to hide her thoughts and impose self-control at the same time; it even gave her a certain pleasure.

She must have felt there was something special about him that very first evening, in the shade of the oleander, the darkness of the podium. Or as they danced: yes, he would know how to awaken her. It seems to me now that it was as plain as day: he moved so differently, so much more supple, as if dancing with him transformed her.

At the beginning everything happened as if it was no more than a one-night stand. Close the curtains, let down her hair, safe gestures, hardened – soon she would no longer have any audience but herself. It almost always began with the same expectation. From a distance, everything seemed possible. Something attracted her to this stranger, the tone of his voice, the way he rolled up the sleeves of his pull-over, revealing his freckled arms. Or his smile, his bright white teeth. Or the stolen glance he had directed towards her. What had actually provoked this response in her, the one she had recognised so well, was unimportant.

The man at the dance had a particular way of running his fingers down her spine. She would first feel a slight shudder grasping her body, then a sudden shiver as if, from now on, she was no longer its sole mistress.

The bed heaved, like a ship.

She lay on it, frozen, waiting.

'Open your eyes,' he said, 'look at me.'

He did not whisper but spoke out loud; she jumped, frightened. She hadn't expected him to speak, no, not now. She obeyed him though. In his expression she saw a reflection of the bedroom, the bed, the light, the shadow, ships at sea, the wind, the music of her own face framed by her hair spread out on the pillow.

She lowered her gaze and saw the long white scar on his shoulder. She could almost reconstruct the operation: the scalpel blade slicing the skin, hesitating twice where the scar twisted.

She saw his chest, smooth like a little boy's.

His flat stomach with a slightly in-turned navel.

As she watched him, she felt him lift her up, turn her over, hold her against him, his face etched with pain, he melted the icy exterior of her marble skin. And suddenly, the spasm. Without warning.

She wanted to stop, to stop him. She said: 'No, no, no . . .' Her voice weak. Her voice flaccid. Desire ebbed and flowed within her like a tide, reaching out and drawing back in purple waves, making her body thrill to a different, secret, forgotten rhythm.

He went to sleep right after.

She turned on her side and leant her head on his arm part of which hung out of the bed, palm up. In the half-light she felt this hand was separate, cut off from the sated body behind her back. She ran her finger from the elbow to the wrist and found the pulse. This man exists, she thought, and his hand is alive. That which she had already renounced had finally occurred. She continued to explore the thick forearm, the solid bones of the wrist, the open palm which seemed made of some other, rougher substance. She already accepted the idea of his departure. He will leave, he will leave, she repeated to herself, folded in on herself as if at any moment someone might hurt her.

There was only one way of keeping him, keeping even the smallest portion of this man lying next to her: to put her palm against his.

Then to go to sleep, keeping in mind the image of this pulse beating regularly beneath the skin.

Beneath his skin. Beneath her skin. When he awakes, all would be different. He would dress quickly. His eyes staring, absent, he would run his hand through his hair, as if unaware of where he was.

But when she woke in the morning, her head was still pressed against his shoulder.

He hadn't gone.

Suddenly there were three of us in the apartment.

She gave me no explanation. She didn't say: 'He is going to stay, that's how it has to be. He's going to live here now, with us. I love him.' She would have been incapable of forming these words, or others, of talking in a way that could make me understand. No words, nothing.

One morning (the morning after the ball? several days later? several months?) I found a shaving case lined with yellow leather on the shelf above the washbasin. It held a gold soap box, a razor, an empty toothbrush case, a comb and a little clothes brush that looked like a toy. A mirror was set into the lid. The boar's hair shaving brush was still wet, standing on the edge of the sink. There was still foam on the round, white shaving soap alongside.

At night, he entered her bedroom.

In the morning he spread his strange objects around the bathroom, in the medicine cabinet, in front of the mirror. Among our towelling robes, our creams, our shampoos, our nail varnish, our hairsprays. When he had finished he left behind his old-fashioned shaving case, the steamed-up window, the dizzying perfume of his aftershave.

A feeling of helplessness flooded through me. I didn't lose my temper, didn't get angry; I felt powerless confronted by his irrefutable presence, this disorder which, before my eyes, transformed itself into order. Confronted by his toothbrush next to ours and the toothpaste tube that he squeezed in the middle.

It's finished, I thought, well and truly finished. He was going to ruin everything, the phoney, lasting armistice that we had established, our way of understanding each other with a gesture, with a glance. He would change my love for my mother, a hungry, exclusive love, intolerant of the presence of a third person, my silent admiration and her way of accepting it. She would no longer smile at me as if, from time to time, she understood me a little.

The floor was pulled from under me: she had no right to do that. Why hadn't she at least warned me that it was him, the man from the open-air dance, who was going to live with us? Why him, in fact, when there had been so many others? No one prepared me for accepting him.

He whose taste of oysters and blood I thought I knew.

The first morning we all had breakfast together. At the other end of the table, as if on a distant horizon, I saw his hand bringing the white porcelain cup decorated with a line of gold to his lips. I saw his mouth rest upon it, his Adam's apple slowly rise and fall as he swallowed, the hairs still wet in the nape of his neck.

She sat opposite him in silence. Without a word she leaned forward to pour him some more coffee. Her hand trembled and the dark liquid suddenly stopped flowing. A drop slid down the white porcelain. He caught it with a finger before it dripped on the cloth.

He licked his forefinger with the tip of his tongue.

I couldn't not see it, the pink tip of his tongue stroking the finger before retreating. I lowered my gaze in excitement. I felt my cheeks blazing and was afraid she would notice – that she would become aware of the tension I feel in his presence. She was going to order me to leave the table, punish me.

But she . . . she didn't look at me. Neither did he. Their eyes were locked together, over the plates, the cups, the breadbasket, the butter dish and the pot of apricot jam which spread a transparent orange shadow across the table.

I didn't exist.

That morning, at that moment, I was not present.

When her eyes finally took me in, it was as if she had been abruptly woken from sleep.

She said: 'In future you will dress before breakfast. I don't want to see you hanging around in your nightdress.'

I noticed then that he too was watching me, that his gaze embraced me, enfolded me. I felt it rest on my shoulders, my neck, my mauve nightdress which, before his eyes, shrank, rode up, slipped, unbuttoned itself, dissolved, fled like quicksilver. His gaze could touch, explore, overturn, looking for an opening, a crack to insinuate itself into and to nestle. Transparent blue eyes which, already on that first morning, made me tremble with desire and fear.

He was her silence, that which she refused to mention, as if bound by oath.

Perhaps you just can't talk about these things, I thought, as his eyes, like the blade of a knife, ran along my neck. He was already inside me, up against me, cleaving to me like on the night of the dance.

His gaze, bewitching, so close.

He smiled.

'Leave her alone,' he said to my mother, buttering a piece of toast.

From that morning on – from that first breakfast illuminated by his presence – she began to change.

She became more flexible, more rounded. Her voice became softer, her movements lighter. Sometimes she sang to herself – when she was alone and I couldn't see her – behind the closed kitchen door as she put away the washing up or cooked the evening meal; she sang: '*Besame, besame mucho, como si fuera esta noche la última vez . . .*' While she sang I felt her becoming more distant, changing from within; I could no longer recognise her.

I was sure that she was escaping from me, that she was heading for undiscovered countries where I could never again be with her.

Fleeing her own solitude I felt she was fleeing me.

But why was she so incapable of saying all that? Why didn't she tell me that just the man's hand brushing against her in passing made her body thrill in anticipation?

I went into the bathroom. The door was open. She was leaning over the bath. The water was running, covering my footsteps. When I touched her shoulder she turned her head without straightening. She looked at me through her lashes, her eyes half closed, like in a trance. She didn't need to open her eyes wide because the only hand allowed to touch her like that was his.

'Mother!'

Her eyes! Her pupils suddenly shrink, her head pulls back and her face reddens.

She hit me.

Not hard. Awkwardly, as if trying to defend herself from her own reflection deep in my eyes. But I felt her fingers burning like fine incandescent steel wires across my cheek.

She turned to the wall and leant her head against the ceramic tiles; I thought she was crying. Through the bathroom window came the noise of someone pulling along a circular washing line, then stopping, then starting again.

'Pass me the clothes-pegs,' a voice cried.

She's going to talk, I thought, she is finally going to say something.

She's going to tell me she has no choice, that the desire he arouses in her tears her apart, like a wound reopening every day. 'Forgive me,' she will say, still turned to the wall, 'forgive me for making you believe that it was dirty, that it was bad . . . I adore his skin, his smell, the taste of his saliva in my mouth. I want him. When we're together I'm not the same person, not the person you are looking at now. I am transformed by his touch. Forgive me,' she will ask, tears running down her magnificent face in a moment of abandon in which she will submit to me utterly.

I would have kissed her cheeks and her wet eyelids.

Her full, salty lips.

She leant against the ceramic tiles, calm, immobile. If she would just turn round. If she would hit me again. If she had really cried, even without words.

But no. Nothing, nothing, nothing.

I wanted to shout, to scream, to utter those words already hanging somewhere, between the noise from the shower and the squeak of the washing line. But I stopped myself. It would have done no good. Separated like this, we understand one another in this tangible solitude, this dumb despair, ineffable, pulsing behind closed eyelids.

Then, still in the bathroom, we watched ourselves losing each other because of him and nothing anyone could do would ever change that, absolutely nothing.

3

He wasn't on my mind as I arrived. I knew there was
no danger of meeting him. He hadn't lived here for
years. Once I left they did stay together for a few
years before splitting up, but I didn't want to know
the whys and wherefores. But when I hung my coat
on a hook in the hall, though, his absence scalded
me.

That particular form of absence: the void.

The empty hook which used to bear his long
camel-hair overcoat smelling of smoke and fog.

The shelf without his grey felt hat.

The hall table without his green plaid scarf and
newspaper folded in four.

Immediately he crossed the threshold he began a campaign of conquest of the place. He put his belongings in our wardrobes, piles of his winter clothes, wrapped up in plastic bags containing mothballs – I knew he had no intention of leaving. He always sat at the same place at table. He left his towels scrunched up on the side of the bath. I found dog-ends everywhere – his presence covered everything with a grey, ashy deposit. He was 'at home', that was plain. Standing in the doorway and glancing round at his conquered possessions, the corridor, the kitchen, the living room, the walls, the carpets, her and me, he seemed to have always lived here. I sometimes thought that soon I would no longer be able to remember a time when he hadn't.

I wanted to be beside her, ever and always closer. His body was an obstacle, a barrier between us. Insidious, threatening, hard. I felt I would have to fight him, day after day. His presence was heavy, suffocating. I bumped against him, against his developing sway over my mother. It caused an ambiguous mixture of excitement and fear to grow in me. When I was close to him I would suddenly get goose bumps, lower my eyes or look away and stutter. He thought I was becoming introverted and sulky. He took hold of my chin and told me it didn't suit me. To try to get around me he had bought me a pair of black poseur high-heeled shoes. She told him: 'They're too old for her.' Then she laughed. It amused her to see him, abruptly, transform me into an adult, into a woman.

She laughed as if it was a game.

'How beautiful she is,' he told her. (Then he added, correcting himself: 'She looks like you.')

He uttered these sentences as if he wasn't talking about me, or as if he thought I was behind some glass wall which prevented me hearing, understanding – an unknown language including and excluding me at the same time.

No, I didn't hate him; he made her more beautiful.

Through the door left ajar I saw her in the morning, standing in front of her mirror, in her short, shiny, honey-coloured négligée. She brushed her hair slowly, still half-asleep, still under the influence of the heat of their bed and of his embrace transforming her. Absently she gazed at her reflected face, looking inwards, the rigid creases slowly melting. She stretched and quickly glanced at her breasts. As she looked, she caressed them, gently.

There was so much sensuality in this look-touch: image of power.

I was jealous of him. He had a power over her that I would never attain.

He's gone. At last. Enormous holes appear where he used to put his things then, spontaneously, memory flows in to fill them.

He is here after all.

Not in the house, but in her and me, when we try to resist him. He is in the furrows he ploughed in us. Threatening, they invade the space, the night which surrounds me. Dawn will soon break. When it is light I will feel safer, I will cope better with his presence in this bedroom – on my skin.

But for the moment, for the moment ... the objects around me bring him bursting back suddenly, they return him to me ... to me, not to her.

Once again I hear him push open the door of the adjacent room – barely audible, only a practised ear would know it. Then his hand, unhesitating, presses my door handle. The door opens and he enters silently. It is dark in the bedroom. The window only lets in a little grey, murky light; it is winter and the dark sky is loaded with low cloud. He stops near my bed. Uncovers me. He slowly lifts the bedclothes so that the abrupt contact with the cold night air will not surprise me, wake me.

Above all he doesn't want to wake me. He just wants to stand by my bed for a while and watch me sleep.

I am motionless, my eyes closed. Not a single movement must reveal to him that I know he is there watching me: I feel his eyes wander over my body, then grasp it to lift it into his arms.

He watches me, sleeping, in the dim grey light. I am lying on my stomach wearing a T-shirt that has ridden up into the middle of my back. The sight of it inflames him and he knows he must go, immediately, leave the room, he must. But he leans forward. For a moment it looks as though he is going to grab the hem of the T-shirt and pull it down over the naked back and protect himself from the desire assailing him. But he changes his mind and presses his lips to my round shoulder, attentive all the while to my breathing. It is regular, peaceful. Gently he pulls the bedclothes back up over my still motionless body. Leaning over like this it seems to him that he sees a fleeting black glimmer as my eyes open – doubtless it was just a twitch of the eyelids, I must be dreaming. He moves away, his shoulders twitching as if he felt the glimmer jag into his back; it will follow him into the other bedroom, the other bed, the other woman who will turn towards him and give herself unreservedly. I lie on my back and sink jerkily into a feverish sleep. I dream that birds are pecking at my stomach and am surprised, in my dream, to find that I don't defend myself: they are hurting me.

I wake up with his kiss still on my shoulder.

When did he touch me for the first time? Was it an accident? Could our first handshake at the end of the ball be considered an embrace, when I thought I already knew him, right down to the taste of his skin? Or was it at the breakfast table when the tip of his tongue licked the drop of coffee from his finger? I shuddered in response, as if it was my own finger.

We were eating dinner. At some point, when she had moved away and couldn't hear, he put his hand on my knee and said:

'I just want to tell you that you are beautiful. Did you know that you are beautiful?'

Red wine glinted in the bottom of the decanter; I thought he had been drinking. He murmured something, then, like someone drunk, he leant forward over his plate of petit pois.

At the same time I felt that my knee accepted his hand, that it nested there.

Suddenly I stood up and the glasses knocked together. She returned at that moment, the salad bowl in her hands, and stopped: she looked at us, looked at the glasses. He was totally concentrated on carefully pushing his petit pois onto his fork with his knife.

Why had no one ever told me until he did?

Why did he pronounce those words like a secret?

Go into my room, look at myself in the mirror.

The mirror didn't come all the way down to the floor. I had to lean forward to see all of myself, to see my legs, foreshortened, strange. This word, 'beautiful', might refer to my body, although . . . not really. It had something unbalanced about it, just like the image reflected back opposite me. I could clearly see that it lacked a dimension still, something that would come from within and impose itself on the world without.

I knew I was missing something just from the way I was examining myself. I was stiff in front of the mirror. My uncertain, almost hesitant, gaze halted a moment on the dark circles around my nipples and just as quickly moved on: I couldn't watch them become erect. Against my will.

Without reason. For a word he uttered and its echo on my skin.

My eye searched for confirmation of his assertion in the mirror. It was a transgression. An identification I desired but which hurt me. He shouldn't have said it lightly, across the dinner table. It seemed impossible to me that some stranger might see me as he saw her, that he should remark it to me, impertinently, as if tossing me a ball to catch.

I didn't know how to assimilate it into my life. Not yet. I took the first step, though. I believed him.

If I had been able to counterbalance his words and my image in the mirror with a childhood memory, solid and irrefutable . . . If I could have escaped, hidden myself in a time where comparison was impossible . . . If I had known how to scratch down deep inside me and find some reminiscence, still doubtless inscribed in the abysses of my body with the visible imprint of his hand resting on my knee . . . There must have been some remains somewhere, some debris that would enable me to erase this sullying touch.

Remember, quickly, remember – but remember what?

The taste of milky semolina? My grazes when I fell off my bike? Piano lessons?

Only one embrace could counterbalance his.

It would have been enough for me to remember her lying next to me to put me to sleep at night – to put to sleep the anxious, grizzling, sensitive child that could only be appeased by her taking it in her arms and squeezing it tight. In my darkened bedroom I wait for her in silence. I listen for her footfall in the corridor. I will only succumb, will only sink into a light sleep when she is close to me, when I feel her sweet touch and smell the glycerine she puts on her hands at night, when she has finished the housework. I will still hear passing cars and distant voices. Then I will breathe more calmly, more slowly, the sign that I am about to sink. Before letting myself go completely, for an instant I will float in a sphere of golden brown crystal. Colours will become clearer, more intense: blue velvet of the shadows, gold light from the corridor filtering through the door left ajar, transparent crystal in which I'm sailing.

The plastic perfection of this image is frightening because of the profound desire it expresses.

It didn't happen like that. I don't know how it was really. I remember nothing. I am incapable of unearthing any memory of her protective touch buried deep inside me, to help defend me from the touch of the man. Find anything, no matter what. An irrefutable sign, proving that I am still just a child, that between he and me there is an impenetrable barrier. But I have nothing more to set against him. The memories of childhood buried in my body sank, hid themselves, got lost when he uttered those words, 'You are beautiful', when he touched me for the first time, when I looked at myself in the mirror. My memories abandoned me at the centre of a new, unknown solitude of a dazzling silver.

Only the smell of the glycerine was true.

The bottle was always balanced on a corner of the sink. In the evening, after washing, she would squeeze a few drops onto the back of her hand, thick, brilliant drops that slowly thinned. With her other hand she rubbed them in. Then she spread the excess that her hands had not been able to absorb on her elbows.

My hands have the same smell this evening. Like her, I add a little lemon juice to the bottle of syrupy transparent liquid. When it touches the glycerine it forms a white scum floating on the surface, then I shake the bottle to mix the two substances together. I rub my hands together for a long time, always the same way, the same as her. My dry skin absorbs the unguent quickly, even round my nails where traces of plaster that the water has not been able to dislodge remain visible.

The smell of lemons sweetens my memories of her.

'Take care of your hands properly after working,' AM would say when I was in her class. And if I didn't follow her advice my palms became so dry that my hands would feel like they were shrinking. She taught that, for a sculptor, after sight, touch was the primary sense. She taught us to distinguish different types of clay, wood and stone blindfold, to differentiate grainy from fibrous structures, to discern the various degrees of heat and resistance of materials (she called it 'expanding the visual consciousness'). She taught us that it is sometimes necessary to entirely subjugate oneself. She had an oval crystal on her desk. As she spoke she passed it from one hand to the other, working it as if she wanted to judge its weight and change its shape at the same time. It might have been to calm her nerves. When people asked her what this object was for she evaded the question: 'Nothing.' But you only had to watch her to know the answer – everyone could see that the crystal was for exercising her fingers.

'Sometimes I think you must be deaf-mute,' she would say to me now and then.

I miss her. I miss her now, as my hands dig into the shadows; the only thing I am able to touch is the past, the past, always the past.

It's pitch black, dark night, moonless. But I don't need to see – the past penetrates me through the ends of my fingers, through my palms, through the mummified skin of my perfectly trained hands.

It billows up from deep inside me.

If only I could have asked some memory from when my father was around for help – summon the tone of his voice or the colour of his shirt buttons that I played with sitting on his lap. A simple memory would have been enough, a straightforward reminiscence, its corners curled up like an old sepia photo. But my memory was dead and I was at its mercy.

As if I was naked.

I was standing in the bath, naked in a great cloud of steam. Perhaps the door wasn't shut, in fact; or maybe he opened it thinking there was no one inside: it makes no difference now. I leant over to grab the towel. First I noticed his shoes on the wet tiles. Then higher, holding the towel. I retreated behind the shower curtain. But he drew it back, turned me towards him and wrapped me in the bath sheet as if afraid I might get cold.

Carefully he dried my back, my shoulders, my belly, my legs – the drops scattered across my skin, one by one.

I didn't resist, I didn't say no.

There wasn't one part of me that could have said no – I couldn't pronounce a sound, a word, I was empty of thought.

Suddenly I turned inside out like a glove, my senses flooded to the surface of my skin, pressed up against his palms, as if it would never again be able to tear itself away.

Only later did the feeling of danger invade that emptiness inside me. The idea of having done wrong assailed me from without, in waves. No, not the idea – it was pain in my stomach caused by all the unuttered warnings that I had interiorised, swallowed long ago and not yet digested. I felt them, intact, wrapped in golden cellophane like chocolates. There, in front of him, the twisted wrappers slowly unwound.

He must have noticed: I stood barefoot, dried by his presence. My muscles seemed to flex to push him away, but he already knew that really I was completely pliant, that I melted beneath his touch.

He didn't move. Me neither. I stood before him, aware of my impotence: my knot of my internal conflicts was already loosening. I knew the danger was no longer as threatening. I had overcome my resistance.

He stood there, calmly waiting. He knew that I wouldn't cry out, that I would say nothing. My habitual silence was transformed into something new – that he read in my eyes and took for desire.

It was the first time I had seen him so close up, him, the man. I felt what she did: tension, something passionate and inflexible emanated from his being, I could breathe it as I stood beside him.

He put his hands on my shoulders. His face bent towards mine. I saw the old scar left by a little cut on his chin coming closer, the lines angling away on each side of his mouth and his watchful grey eyes, coming closer and closer.

That's how she sees him, I thought, and slipped my hand in between his lips and mine before they could meet.

But the kiss passed right through.

There was a knock at the door.

She was going to come in, catch us in this prohibited act, my raised hand, him, dangerously close. She would see his tightened muscles, the way he leant forward: one body gently bending over another. She would see the uncertain shudder of my head. Finally she would notice that I burn up when he touches me, as she stands there, watching me.

I would see her as she stands there, dumb-founded, next to us, as she imagines herself in my position, recognising her mute bewilderment, her powerlessness, her own capitulation.

For the first time a hint of true anxiety would appear on her pale lips.

I couldn't stand the idea that she might be afraid of me.

Or maybe she would come in without even glancing at him. As if he wasn't there. Or as if it had no importance. She would contemplate me, naked in the puddle of water streaming down the drain in the centre of the bathroom floor. I would stand between them, alone, adult suddenly, naked. I would say to her: 'Ask me what happened.' With a wave of the hand she would still my voice and ask him, him. He would say the girl had provoked him, leaving the door open when she takes a bath. Then she'd bend down, pick up the towel and tell me: 'Cover yourself.'

Her voice would sound like a heavy object falling to the floor.

A moment when she didn't open the door, when I was afraid she would open it, had passed. A little later I breathed a sigh of relief seeing that the key had been turned in the lock. I knew that this moment of shared anxiety sealed an agreement between him and me, between my body and his.

I didn't go and see her. I didn't tell her what had happened. Alone in the bathroom I swallowed up those words.

Something new was bubbling up inside me. The secrets I had to hide multiplied, intersected. I could no longer go back. I had no other exit. I know now that it was possible to interpret my silence as acceptance – for him that's what it was, a sort of calm resignation, this lack of voice, this lack of a cry. I kept silent in the bathroom. I kept silent when he came into my room for the first time. I would remain silent later, all that winter.

Not a word, not a sound, nothing.

I was woken by hot kisses on the soles of my feet. I didn't move and pretended to be asleep like before. I buried my head in the pillow to stop my breathing from betraying me – furtive sighs, the racing pulse of my blood. He knelt by my bed and put his head on the pillow. He stroked my hair, several times. 'Wake up,' he murmured, 'wake up.' Through my lashes I saw his face close to mine and a ribbon of light crawling across the opposite wall. The rest of the room remained plunged in darkness, black like the voice penetrating me, trying to force open the final gateway.

He doesn't understand that if I wake, if I speak, I will lose her.

Because she will wake up too. She will hear my voice on the far side of the wall – if I cry out, if I sigh, if I moan. Even if I laugh. She won't think that I am in danger. She will instantly guess what is happening. She will curl up in her bed and wait for the noise to cease. She will die a little with each echo that reaches her from my room.

Don't wake up, clench your teeth. Let the hands mauling me once again continue in silence.

Still kneeling, he slipped a finger under the elastic of my knickers, between the skin on my thigh and the material. He pulled, as if testing its strength. All at once I was frightened. I rolled over to the far side of the bed, up against the wall. He snatched his hand away (that part of my skin suddenly became chilled). He remained still for a moment, expectant. Then, carefully, he lay down next to me.

He was behind me then, breathing calmly, as if asleep. I lay on my side. He folded his legs into mine, their hairs tickling me pleasantly. Again I pretended to move in my sleep. He clung to me, certain I wouldn't wake up, that I didn't want to wake up. Tenderly he stroked my stomach, a furtive touch meaning: Don't be frightened, everything is OK, it's only me, you've known me for ages, and I alone can teach you about your beauty.

Gently, for fear that some ill-considered gesture might disturb the harmony of the moment, he rolled me onto my back and placed a hand upon my breasts. He didn't slide it under my nightdress, just rested it on top. Without pressing, as if he wanted to feel my heartbeat.

Then lightly pressing with his palm he described a circle around my nipple.

That was all.

I didn't move. I wasn't frightened but there beside him I became an amorphous mass. I decomposed. His presence caused a strange confidence to grow inside me: it seemed that I became aware, remotely somehow, that I needed his hands to teach me to feel my body, to discover what I was – a boiling void coated with some substance which his hands could shape into a woman. A little like I might model a clay figure. My thumbs and my wooden spatula must give a form to this indeterminate object, this dark, fat, sweating earth. I feel it submit to my fingers, I become aware of my power.

His hands were like mine – two separate beings, completely cut off from the rest of his body. I only recognised this much later – this thrill in the hands – when I start work on a new piece, as I approach the material, wood or clay. Impatient to touch, to feel, to make it submit to my palm.

I am frightened of stone. I remember my nausea when the block of marble, weeping a glacial fluid, was delivered to my studio. For several days I just walked round it. I felt revolted, as if some secret forces combined to form a magnetic field around it on the ground, a virtually impenetrable circle.

As if the block knew which body I wanted to sculpt.

As if she was already inside, even before the first blow of my chisel.

Sometimes he didn't even touch me. His hand firmly gripped mine and guided it like a blind child. He wanted to teach me what a body is. We slid together down the chest, over the hips, the belly, and lower. Along this unknown flesh, both mine and alien. 'Now you, do it yourself,' he told me. I obeyed his whispered orders, I didn't dare protest against the pleasure awaiting me. My body reacted to my own caresses, not his. I heard his heavy breathing behind me, the only sign of his presence beside me.

'I love your body,' he said, holding me tight against him.

There was something obscene in his words.

I have not yet been able to come to terms with this word. I would like to tell him that I don't want to be a body. The body is made of blood. The body is her trailing after me, mopping up the traces of blood I scatter as I pass. I would like to awake once and for all from this deceptive, slightly protective sleep and tell someone everything – but it is too late, it is already too late. A spasm convulses me. I curl up pressing my forehead against the wall. In the darkness I seek out a little hole I have scratched with a fingernail level with my head. I slip the end of my forefinger into it and scratch, further, deeper. The finger digs down into the crumbling, disintegrating plaster. It's a pleasant sensation, as if all of me was contained in this finger, as if it was all of me hiding in the wall, in the dark, round shelter, surrounded by lumps of white limestone, grains of grey sand and powdery cement. I feel safe here. When I have dug deep enough, I lick my forefinger and scrape the plaster out from under my finger-nail with my teeth: the wall tastes refreshing.

All this time his hand runs up and down my spine, as if he understands how hard it is to accept oneself. I stay still until his palms have finally relaxed the stiff muscles in my neck and shoulders. Then I sink once more into a trembling, intoxicating half-sleep.

Later I waited for him, excited, ready.

At night he wasn't roughly male, like during the day. His caresses were tender, burning, as if he was no longer the man who lived with my mother, no longer my stepfather with the ringing laugh and striped shirts, who took a nap after lunch and passed me the salt at the dinner table. His nightly being was invisible, but I couldn't escape him. In our relationship flight was inconceivable. Not now, not after having kept silent for so long.

I couldn't subtract myself from myself, because his presence was my only signpost towards my bodily essence.

The distance between our bodies narrowed. There was less and less room for words. I still closed my eyes, however. I waited, lying in total darkness. But for my skin all my senses were as if anaesthetized. Sometimes it was hard. When his lips seized my nipples for the first time I thought I wouldn't be able to stop myself from crying out. Doubtless he noticed; I had to bite my lip, emit a strangled sound on the border of a cry. Quickly he placed his lips on mine. I pushed him away without a word. He understood: his mouth went back to the nipple and I thought he was going to eat me, that it was over, that he was going to eat me right up. I was going to wake up breastless, bellyless, gnawed, with bloody holes where my bosom should be. And she would see.

She couldn't do otherwise. No.

The thought that she would discover everything pushed me further towards him.

Not for a moment, however, did I forget that she was there with us, within arm's reach. Just a thin brick partition wall separated the different cadences of our breath from hers. When I managed to calm myself a little, I heard her turn over in her sleep. The bed creaked – slight squeak of the wood, like a whine. As if she was whimpering.

Lying in her double bed she suspects nothing yet. She sleeps.

I imagined we were alone once more and that it was me, not him, who lay down next to her. My body would stretch out alongside hers, in the same position, the same curves, the same shadowy hollows. Our double form. I would touch her as he touches me. She would be half asleep and her skin would prickle, her breathing accelerating. Worried, she would turn towards me. 'You see,' I would tell her, 'our bodies are like animals; they wake up the same way. The same thing happens in me when he touches me: my blood circulates differently, flooding to the surface of my skin, whirling and warming beneath his fingers.'

Not yet awake, she would dream: she is swimming in the sea and notices her shadow on the white, sandy seafloor – her hidden side, her dark side.

I would tell her: 'The man's touch weaves bonds between us.'

Each time he left my room, now, I found it easier to cope with the idea that he was going to her, that he touched her, that he woke her with a kiss which still held the taste of my skin, that he rested his palms on her, still smelling of me. She wakes up, grabs his hands and brings them to her cheeks. For a moment she halts, baffled, disturbed by this salty, saturated odour that she doesn't recognise . . . But it only lasts a moment, so much does it resemble her own. As she soaks up this perfume, transported by his hands, we are closer than we have ever been before.

Only the man's skin separates us.

I think that now I could open the door of their bedroom and slip into their bed next to them. What would be so strange? I know both of them. I would lie on her side and bury my face in the hollow of her shoulder. I would push away her hair to reveal the little patch of naked skin behind her ear. My tongue would feel it, speckled with little invisible hairs.

She would turn slowly towards me and I would stretch out my hand towards her breast. My hand would meet hers. My lips would find hers. Her gaze would meet mine. She would be there, squeezed between our equally voracious bodies, possessed, powerless before our desire.

Each time pleasure came into my thoughts, I felt I would have to die. I felt that I was giving my hand to death, my single, invisible sister.

If I had died then – suddenly, in my sleep – my mother would never have known anything. Broken, exhausted by weeping, she would once more have lowered over her pale face and austere bun – a provocative austerity – the black veil that suited her so well. Perhaps it would have been easier for her to kiss my cold, dry forehead, absently to stroke my cheeks, than to learn what had been going on on the other side of the wall.

I was sure I was going to die. Because I had said nothing to her.

One can die of it. Of silence.

Around the beginning of spring he stopped coming. Feverish I listened out for the slightest noise, the door opening, his well-known step. I soon gave up and sank in sleep, from which I awoke drenched, rent, afflicted.

Like now I curled into the wall in the dark. I tried to hear his voice, lying in wait for the words that would explain his absence, the echo of an argument. Had she heard then? Had he confessed? Had she guessed? From my eyes? From my behaviour? Had she noticed my transformation, my desire to look more and more like her? I tried to walk, to talk, to sit like her. Sometimes she would examine me fixedly, as if becoming aware of the similarity and fearing that he should see it.

How I wished someone would give me the answers to the questions I couldn't ask.

I anticipated some sign, anything, a gesture, an unfinished sentence that would reveal the sense of his actions. But beneath the thin crust of everyday life I could discern nothing.

He still sat at the same place at table, in the uncertain spring sunbeams; he offered me a piece of fruit or my favourite ice cream, vanilla chocolate chip. All as if nothing had happened. Everything had taken place at night. Night things didn't exist. I sit opposite him shovelling great mounds of ice cream into my mouth so as not to scream.

It took me a long time to understand that this was, precisely, the sign I was looking for, this routine behaviour which said: Everything is fine. He reads the paper. She leans against him and a lock of her hair strokes his cheek. He turns towards her and says something. She laughs. Laughs. Laughs. It seems to me that she will never stop.

Once again I am excluded, beyond the circuit of their eyes, of their gestures.

Once more, I don't exist.

I want to brush aside this lock of hair and tell her everything, slowly, make her understand at last. But it is more dangerous to talk to her than to touch her.

I perceived a trace of suspicion, of anxiety, all the same. One day she was looking for something in my

wardrobe and found a present he had given me
which I had hidden in a drawer of clothes I didn't
wear any more – a black suspender belt. She didn't
put it back in the same place. Rummaging around
at the bottom of the drawer she discovered the little
paper bag. For a moment she wondered if she
should open it – why be suspicious, see secrets
everywhere? But a piece of black lace was unfolding
already in her fingers and she saw the pretty suspender belt with three little satin roses stitched into
the front.

It's not hers, it can't be hers, she thought. Then
she removed from their packet a pair of long black
stockings which had plainly been worn.

She could no longer disguise the truth.

'She wears them, she puts them on,' she said,
flabbergasted, without even noticing that she is
speaking out loud.

She imagines her daughter, naked, on the edge
of a chair, carefully removing the stockings from
the bag. She hears her open the packet in the afternoon silence. Then her daughter licks her fingers
with the tip of her tongue and puts them on, tossing her great mane of hair back as she does so.
Slowly she stretches them. Then she gets up. Adjusts
the suspender belt on her naked body. Leans over
to attach the hem of the stocking. Takes the dress
from the back of the chair. Puts it on. Feels the

warm material on her belly, on the skin of her thighs. As she moves about the room the fabric caresses her like a man's hands, prudent, as yet undecided: the dress spins and flares, clings, feels, retreats, brushing now the stockings, now the skin.

In the street she is suddenly aware of the stifling heat: welling up from the asphalt, emanating from the pavement, rising like a tide, enveloping her legs, above the hem of her stockings. Sweat pearls at the place where her thighs rub together in walking. The whole lower half of her body is dominated by the street. The thin summer dress sticks to her damp skin, a line becomes visible where the lace of the suspender belt stops on the naked arch of her belly. She goes into a dark hallway and the chill air washes down over the outsides of her legs. Her body cools down.

But she is still burning inside. The heat of the asphalt seems to have stored itself away in her centre of gravity.

On the third floor she presses a doorbell impatiently. The strident ring makes her jump. She stands on the landing. She thinks she may give up – turn round and walk away, take off the suspender belt and the stockings. Erase everything, forget everything – this expectation, this tension in the guts, this stormy afternoon, the overheated air vibrating against her body . . . But the door opens and, without a word, she throws herself on the bed, in the shadowy bedroom smelling of withered flowers. She is short of breath. She tries to curl up, to turn on her side. She is afraid of herself, of this awareness of self that takes hold of her. But it is no longer possible. Her body no longer obeys her. It is no longer her own. It is no longer only her own.

He approaches. His face unseen.

He lifts the dress that sweat sticks to her and reveals the lower part of the woman's body, her flesh sheathed with black. He pulls the large skirt up over the torso, the face, they disappear beneath it like a shroud.

The fabric rises slightly, the solitary clue proving that this half is alive, that it exists.

He looks at her. She doesn't see him.

She feels on her skin the path taken by his gaze.

Rough like a tongue.

At last the man moves away and opens the window wide. In the light that inundates the room her flesh is dazzling, blinding.

My mother stands in the middle of the bedroom, the stockings in her hand. This hallucination maddens her, the whiteness of the skin contradicting the black lingerie: duplicity. Her hands tremble as she opens the drawers one after another. The suspender belt which evoked the vision is not enough for her. She looks for something more, some more atrocious, more disgusting secret. She rummages in the carefully folded clothes, slides her hand under the sheets and feels, in her chest, the rapid, surreptitious beating. As if an alien heart was beating inside her.

She finds nothing.

She halts a moment, her hands empty, alone in the silent bedroom. Then she grabs the desk drawer and hurls it to the floor. It crashes noisily to the ground. An old stamp album falls out and a picture of a strange bird, found in a bar of chocolate called 'The Animal Kingdom', a pen, a pencil sharpener, plasticine, some dried out chewing gum and an orange diary. The diary opens at the page where a photo of her child has been stuck. Three years old. Holding a little oval mirror in one hand and a comb in the other. It seems as if it is only now that she realises, faced with this picture, that the child coquettishly doing its hair is a girl.

She almost tears the photo to shreds.

She is suffocated by the idea that this same little girl, a few years later, will teasingly put on a black suspender belt and go to a rendezvous she has arranged with a man. She approaches the wardrobe. Opens it. Takes out all the clothes hanging there: the lambskin winter coat, the leather jacket, the grey raincoat, the brushed cotton blazer with its shiny elbows (what a lot of useless old things, she thinks in passing), the plaid wool blouse, the dress decorated with cherry-coloured rep . . . A combination of the lavender and the green ribbons soaked in some liquid used to discourage moths wafts across the bedroom. God knows how long they had been crushed in the back of the now-empty wardrobe. They are completely faded. Suddenly she feels her cheeks are wet. She wipes away her tears and then, with damp palms, she picks up the belongings made heavier by her feeling of guilt and puts them away. It's stupid, she thinks. These images haunting me have no existence outside my imagination. I am constantly on the alert. I am always frightened. I am suspicious of everything. The suspender belt is perhaps just the harbinger of something yet to happen. Nothing is yet certain.

It comes to her that her daughter no longer has long hair and that she therefore can't toss it backwards as she pulls on her stockings.

Yes, it's just a hallucination. It's me I am seeing dressing, walking down the street in a clinging dress beneath which I am only wearing a suspender belt and stockings. This thought frees her of her nausea yet burdens her, crushes her at the same time.

Something in this phantasmagorical image vexes her however: she recognises the suspender belt. He gave her exactly the same one with roses embossed on the front. Pure coincidence, she says to herself, repressing this thought even before it is conceived. She is too afraid it will become reality if ever she formulates it.

She feels disgust consuming her. The bitterness of suspicion collects in her throat. She stands in the middle of my bedroom, but thinks of herself. She sees herself as I am incapable of seeing her because I can never come close enough: she notices new crow's feet around her eyes, perceives that her muscles no longer know how to relax, that a tiredness of which she was previously unaware tenses them.

She sees herself from within, contemplates the inside of her skin, the wrinkles yet to form, the scars that will only become visible to other people once more time has passed. Unconsciously she straightens her shoulders and runs her fingers over the skin, still smooth and tight.

Still.

She already thinks in those terms. Age is infiltrating her.

'She is making me old,' she says out loud, even though she is only talking to herself. 'Just the idea that she could be carrying on with a man deforms me. I disintegrate inside.'

She thinks about her age as a constraint imposed from without: thirty-six. Blinding, dazzling naked skin on the bed. Not her skin.

At that moment she alone knows how much she has been worn away inside.

The suspender belt still lies on the floor. She picks it up, incredulous, and smiles as if seeing it for the first time. How had she not thought of it before? The solution was there at her feet, the answer to the questions that torture her. Suspenders. Her daughter had sewn white rubber suspenders onto it. It's like drinking champagne from a plastic cup, she thinks, reassured, and brings them closer to her face to scrutinise them. She is satisfied now, she understands. The fact that her daughter attached white suspenders to a black suspender belt explains everything: it couldn't be serious. Yes, that's it, white suspenders on a black belt – she's still a child! What other explanation could there be? How otherwise can you explain these two incompatible things? That's not how to go about it, she wants to shout at her, you don't seduce a man with white suspenders hanging off a black suspender belt, it's ridiculous. She laughs but her guilt becomes twice as heavy, making the bedroom suffocatingly airless. She opens the window. Let in the outside reality, these noises filling her emptiness, bringing her back to herself: a child crying, a dog barking, the distant hum of the street. Someone in her neighbourhood is practising their violin lesson. The sound of the musical instrument wakes her completely. As she goes out she glances back at the room. She sees the mess, clothes folded on a chair, the bed unmade, the wardrobe open. Without reason she drops her gaze and stares at her bright red varnished toenails. She thinks the varnish on her right big toe is chipped, that she has been letting herself go. She wonders if that is the root of everything.

I still didn't speak. Mute, I swallowed days saturated with dumb, inscrutable gazes and sleepless nights.

The waiting and the silence flowing through my veins like molten lead made me ill. I was in bed, wiped out, separated from my body. I pushed it away, I wanted to punish it for having betrayed me. It stayed in bed whole days, abandoned, dispossessed, bereft of sense.

Leaning over the bowl I sicked up great jets of vomit. The blue enamel rim disfigured, drifted out of my field of vision. At night I wailed in fear and begged them not to turn out the light. I tried to get up but my feet refused to advance. I strained to speak. Instead of speech a yellowish fluid mixed with saliva spurted out of my mouth. Then once again the blue edge of the bowl. It advanced on me, followed me, tightened my throat, harder and harder. I heard myself gagging.

Only silence and darkness did me good.

I am in bed; the bedroom is dark like a closed oven. I am so exhausted by the fever and the vomiting that my jaw trembles when I try to sit up against the pillows. I still cannot speak. I am emptied, scraped out inside. Only the others' existence persuades me that I am real: I hear voices outside, footfalls, music on the radio. Her voice. 'It has to stop sometime,' she says. She leans over me, listening to my panting breath. Her lips press against my forehead.

Sweet, cool touch. Like new.

'My poor child, you're burning up.'

I understand the word 'child', shining for a moment in front of my eyes before disappearing into the blackness, an incandescent red ball.

Abruptly I start to get better. Huge drops of sweat appear on my forehead, roll down my neck, my breasts, my belly. Previously something in the air in the room stopped the sweat from forming. I no longer tremble. The fever drops. I wake from a long, cloying nightmare. Once more it is night, but another night, a gentle spring night that I recognise because it is not hostile to me. My mother picks up the bottle of alcohol. Removes the nightdress stuck to my body, then lingeringly, her hands dampened, she rubs my forehead, my neck, my back, my legs, my feet.

At last, the touch of her hands.

I feel that each of her gestures frees me a little from the slurry of sticky, wet plaster which has been enveloping and clutching me like a mould. Her powerful hands rebuild me. With an instinctive assurance she models the burning, feverish mass into a body again. Me. She sculpts it as she would like to see it: she cleaves the muscles back onto the bones, relocates the joints, straightens the arms and legs.

I abandon myself to the beatitude of my weight-less body.

She doesn't touch my breasts. She avoids them as if they didn't exist. Under her hands I become a child once more – her child.

I place a kiss on her palm. Smell of alcohol.

Perhaps I should do the same thing now. Go into her room, sit by her bed, turn down the bedclothes and massage her swooned, sleeping body with alco-hol. But I am frightened that she will flinch from my touch, withdraw into her shell. She will never give up the bedclothes, the debris, the obstacles that have built up between us.

There is a wall between us.

Behind the newly pasted wallpaper someone must have filled the hole I scratched in the plaster. Nevertheless, sitting there, propped up by pillows, I recognise the wall. In return it recognises my back, the way I plant my feet firmly down onto the floor, as if I was preparing to dive. Then the wall gives way sometimes, becomes softer, thinner, transparent. I hear and see what is happening beyond, like in a mirror.

Pieces of past events, snatches of old silence.

I cling to it as long ago. I press my face tight against it and wait.

I listen. The wall remains silent, as before.

I put the ashtray on my knees. Only the incandescent ember of my cigarette is alive in the disturbing black velvet silence. Slowly it moves in an arc from my knees to my mouth. Then it starts wavering, guttering jerkily. As if a powerful spasm was shaking my limbs, my lips.

Fear. Fear remains.

Noise of the ashtray falling to the floor. The cigarette goes out.

4

I opened her bedroom door. I want to hear her wake up. When she opens her eyes I will be close to her – so close that my face will fill her entire field of vision.

Being close to her. Feeling her gaze on my face.

I'm not afraid she'll die. Not for a moment have I considered this possibility. It's something else: I feel lost. I've lost her. I no longer know who she is, I don't recognise her. It's plain as day, there, standing in the doorway, on the threshold, not yet inside, plunged in complete, deafening silence. I feel I have never seen her laid so bare, so absent from herself. The bedside lamp standing on the bedside table is veiled with a scarf inside which light is draped in darkening folds; the bedroom seems wrapped in some transparent cloth. She lies motionless, covered only by a sheet. She breathes slowly, her breast scarcely rising. Before my eyes the shape of her body suddenly appears hard and clear, precise like a sculpture, and I perceive the stone beneath. I see her, I see her breathing. Waiting. Waiting for my hands to bring her back to life.

But I am tired from travelling, from my sleepless night. I'm drained with remembering.

I've had enough of her, of this house, of myself.

I stand on the threshold and weariness crashes over me like a wave. It takes up residence in my hands, in my shoulders, in my neck. The more I look at her the more my neck muscles tighten and ache. I know this defeating burden, this special form of impotence. It comes from handling the chisel and the mallet. Marble dust sparkles in the winter sun. The path of my steps – my indecision – is clearly traced around the plinth. The chisel slips down the angled face of the block without cutting it, disobeying me, leaving a smooth, soapy trail on the stone.

She is inside. She is breathing.

Through my chisel, my gloves, my skin, I feel her furtive gestures, her shivers, her fear of the blow reaching her at last, well before its recoil strikes me. White with dust, trembling, stiff, as if I am part of the statue. That I am its hidden, mobile aspect. At one moment, no longer able to stand the pain in my shoulders, exhausted, I say: 'I give up.' I think this is still possible. But no, not any more.

Watching her sleep now, weak, on the point of death, drowned in the impotence of the body and the whiteness of the sheet – my determination, my blows seem to me so very senseless.

I lean on the door frame and reflect that that is all history: my combat, my victory, everything, except the tenacious memory of the effort, buried deep in my flesh. All that remains to me is the desire to be close to her and the insidious fear that this might not be possible. No, not here, not in this bedroom. Not in the same bedroom.

I am still frightened to go in. Every particle of me rebels. Hear the door closing behind me. The sound of the key turning quietly. Then footsteps. Silence and footsteps.

Approaching.

That day I went into her room. As soon as I had crossed the threshold I smelt the breath of her perfume floating high up near the ceiling. The window was open. The curtains exhaled an odour of cotton and damp which, each night, oozed from

123

the exterior wall, infiltrated the room and clung to the thick folds of lace. It must have been midday. From the courtyard I could hear children's voices and the murmur of falling rain.

The bed was unmade, its white guts exposed. I threw myself onto it face down and buried my face in the pillow smelling of camomile, shampoo and face powder. Underneath it my hand came upon a scrunched up handkerchief. Beneath my fingers I felt the fine cambric hemmed with a silk band. It had her smell – sweat wiped from her forehead at night when she is startled awake from a dream where an unknown masked man strangles her, lingeringly, slowly. I rolled the handkerchief into a ball and kept it for a while in my hand: impossible to be closer to her. Since he invaded our home she had escaped me. She told me it wouldn't be a bad idea for me to attend school in another town, that it would get me out and about. I wouldn't spend all my time shut up in my room.

She said that I would have more freedom. I saw nothing but her lips emerging from her face. The word 'freedom' was just a pair of empty syllables proffered by her made-up, half-open mouth, that sweet fleshy circle.

As she pronounced the word, I felt she was printing it on my face, on my breasts, on my neck. My skin received the bright red brand.

Freedom. How round it was, this word, how damp and hot in her mouth.

I lay on her side of the bed. On the other side the smell was not the same. It was the man's, penetrating, saturated. Threatening to invade the whole room.

Suddenly I felt he was there. He crept up behind, he burst in. I heard his furtive steps, the parquet creaking beneath his feet. I lay motionless – in that deaf house, in that mute bedroom. Exposed once more.

He must have been there for some time. He had no doubt heard me come in and had hidden, waiting.

It was no longer a question of satisfying the expectation and hope silting me up like alluvium throughout that spring up until my illness. Until summer. I thought I had purged myself through sweating and vomiting, that I had exorcised the desire of the flesh that he had accustomed me to, night after night. My skin had become so fine, so sensitive, so vulnerable that I felt it would tear if ever he touched me again.

I shan't cry out, I thought. The beating of my heart made me suddenly deaf. I'm going to pretend to be asleep once more. In any case she isn't there . . . she's never there.

The courtyard is silent now. It has stopped raining. I lie facing the window and gaze round the bedroom inundated with sunlight. The luminosity accentuates the whiteness of the walls.

The sudden calm was ill-omened, somehow, and in the light piercing the clouds and shafting into the bedroom, delivering me up to his gaze, to him.

His step is firm now.

His body pushes before it a wave of heat that assaults me, searing my back even before he touches me. The front of my body is quite cold.

Violently he turns me over to face him. I open my mouth to utter what is tearing me up inside: foreboding of misfortune, fear. My cry, so long held back, is finally going to erupt and liberate me of his presence.

But then I see his hand close up against my face, his fingers fanned out, bent, closing on it, gagging me. I choke. It's over, finished. His touch takes my breath away; beneath my eyelids deep, dark red chasms are wheeling.

He relaxes his grip. Close up his skin smells of her, her smooth hips, her breasts, her hair. But the smell of camomile wafting up from her pillow is stronger. I feel the taste of his palm on my lips then my tongue slips, as if it didn't belong to me, as if it had been torn out of me, over the rough back of his hands, between his fingers. They no longer clutch my face. He pushes them into my mouth

126

and trembles with desire to touch inside me. Once he has touched the wet mucous membranes he will know all about me.

I bite and lick his fingers at the same time.

With his other hand he clutches my hair and pulls my head back. Then his lips press against my neck; it resists, trembles, still inhabited by the cry. But now the cry has another meaning, unknown, terribly dangerous.

The room heaves, transparent with luminosity. Light assaults us from every side – he and I together in daylight for the first time.

We are revealed. Done for. She sees us. She is somewhere in the house spying on us in silence.

My silence and hers close in on him, a perfect circle.

'Leave me alone,' I say quietly, my voice hoarse, injured by his caresses.

He holds me tighter. All at once I let myself go against his burning skin. Nothing has any importance any more besides this heat that invades me. Now I can clearly distinguish their two odours, his and my mother's. They weave into one another and catch me in their net. I do not try to defend myself.

My cry expires in the hollow of his mouth, between his tongue and his palate.

It is no longer a cry of fear.

His body is above me, simultaneously frightening and close at the same time. On his chest I recognise the place she noticed through the neck of his sky-blue shirt on the evening of the dance.

The place where I wanted to sink my teeth.

The time gone by since then disappears, is devoured. I am back there once more and I hate the wind, the cloth, the skin separating us. The black silk of her dress, the net bodice shaping her bosom, my white cotton dress, his shirt – all this superfluousness hindering us, preventing us from hurling ourselves headlong into the maelstrom of desire.

I bit him. My teeth sank into his skin. Taste of his body that I guessed a long time ago: smooth warmth I could drink in till I lose consciousness. He writhes, retreats and penetrates me brutally as if by this act liberating himself once and for all from some unknown pain that has accumulated inside him.

At that moment I thought we were alike.

We formed a single being, she and I. The man's body explored our enclosed intimacy and ran aground, deep, deep within us, there, where we are the same.

How to breach the door now, still the obstacle planted at the threshold of the bedroom. How to relax this tightening in the throat?

The man is still between us. Him. Absent, forgotten, dismissed, cursed. He is there again, separating our bodies, spoiling our reunion. Between our naked skin and our clothing. Filling the voids he inevitably finds in us.

The spaces between.

I feel him, his hands, his breath. He hides behind the wardrobe, or inside it, in among the clothes. I see him in the creaky keyhole, in the steam on the bathroom window, in the shreds of tobacco at the back of the drawer.

Our bodies are nests for his absence. He expands, overflows out of me and walks around the apartment. I notice his shadow in the corridor. There he is going into the kitchen, putting on the light and heating water to make coffee. I couldn't make any yesterday. She doesn't buy it any more, because of him. She couldn't dissociate its aroma from his smell, heat consuming her as she touched the cup, as she took her first swallow each morning.

Nausea wells up in me as I touch the cup of tea. It's not yet time to go into the room, sit on the side of the bed and say to her: 'Wake up.'

Just now, in the kitchen, the cup of tea in my hand, I saw her again as I did that afternoon. She had just come in from shopping and started getting dinner ready straight away. Her movements lively, decisive. She sorted the yellow shucks of peas from the new potatoes, put a saucepan of water on the gas and lit the oven for the joint. Then she cut up a lettuce and put it to soak in a bowl of cold water. The kitchen grew too small for her abrupt movements. I grabbed a green apple from the table. It was smooth and shiny as if covered in wax.

She still hadn't faced me.

I gazed past the apple at the floor and my bare feet. I muttered the word: rape.

She turned off the tap and, with her hands still in the sink, she turned towards me as if she had misheard.

'I beg your pardon.'

I had to raise my eyes, look her in the face.

'He assaulted me,' I said, even more quietly, and bit into the apple as if biting into my own voice.

She said nothing. She clung to the sink, all her weight in her shoulders and her arms. Her gaze rested upon me, then wandered away, into the shadowy corridor dimly lit by a strip of light that crept under the bedroom door at the end. I saw her eyes that darkened then emptied. Her fury, like a bloated, threatening wave, was about to be unleashed, inundating the kitchen, the corridor, creeping under the door, filling the bedroom to the ceiling – deadly maybe – then withdrawing, soothed, placated.

'I don't believe you,' she said.

Only then did she turn to look at me. She frowned a little. In her eyes I saw that something about me disturbed her. What was it she didn't like? My scraped-back hair, still wet, my T-shirt, my bare feet, the apple in my hand? I thought that a detail like that wouldn't have made her pause, not at this moment. My appearance, my clothes. What did it matter whether I was wearing a dress, a T-shirt or a nightdress? When her gaze, filtered by the 'I don't believe you', finally reached me, I said to myself that perhaps, in a way, she was right.

I shouldn't have announced it to her like that, so abruptly. There was something wrong in all this: my clothes, my voice, the draught in the corridor, the distant sound of music. She didn't understand. Everything was normal. How could she have anticipated what I had to tell her? She had been shopping. In the crowd she stepped on someone's toes. She bought a joint and a lettuce. Then, as she waited for the tram, she noticed a familiar face reflected in a shop window. The man passed close by her. She didn't turn round. A smell of fresh bread hung in the tram. She came home and started cooking. Her fourteen-year-old daughter burst in behind her and, mumbling between two mouthfuls of apple, told her that her stepfather had raped her.

She grasps her handbag and takes out a mirror. She smooths a stray lock of hair.

'I don't believe you.'

I shouldn't have washed. I should have gone to her crying, with a cut lip and streaks of blood on my thighs, fragments of his skin beneath my fingernails. But I had restored everything. I had tidied the bedroom. Had a bath. Erased all trace. Just as she had always taught me – leave no trace.

At first she hadn't heard. Now she didn't understand. My words had bounced off her face back into my mouth where, like the apple, my teeth ground them up before they descended into my stomach.

She is making herself busy round the kitchen again. I notice the tension in her shoulders, her slow, stiff movements. I decide it isn't a good sign – this hardness, this rigidity – she hasn't yet grasped what has happened, she doesn't understand that while she was out this man . . . It's flabbergasting: she's carrying on peeling potatoes, being careful not to cut too deeply into the flesh. She's thinking about something else. What she did in town. The heat. She rinses the lettuce leaves one by one beneath the powerful jet of water. She is lost in thought, her actions slow, calm. For a moment I too feel that nothing has really happened. The tap is running, steam raises the lid of the saucepan on the stove. The oven is making the kitchen hotter and hotter. Between the distinct noises in the room and the more remote noise of the street I seem to perceive snatches of threatening silence. But the regular beating of my heart and the pleasant sharpness of the apple crunching beneath my teeth reassure me.

The sky is cloudy once more. It is raining.

I should have told her nothing.

Just before I spoke, before the words, like sparks, leapt across the space between us, while they were still searing my throat, I felt that she wouldn't survive the revelation. She will never get over it, I said to myself, choked with the irresistible desire to talk to her, to tell her, once and for all, to no longer be so alone in thrall to my body. She will collapse, speechless, floored by my words. When I lean over her she will suddenly notice, like through a magnifying glass, the traces he left on my skin. The purple love bite on my neck. The circular bruises from his fingers round my wrists. The scratch on my shoulder. She will think she's dying then. She will feel the injuries invading her. neck, bony fingers digging into her throat, deep, down into her lungs.

If I came right up close to her, if I showed her, perhaps she would see past words. She would examine me whole. She wouldn't recognise my face because of the red mist veiling her eyes and the noise in her chest and head. Perhaps she would scream: 'You bitch!'

Suddenly I want her to hit me, to lacerate my face with her fingernails. Or embrace my shoulders, the same shoulders that at any moment will be shaken by sobs.

She can chastise me now, impose one of those punishments with which for years she silently threatened me as she washed the blood from the tiles behind me, from the sheets, from hands. How can I tell her that before he arrived I didn't exist? How can I describe to her this feeling of non-life, this deprivation of the body? Being so absent from oneself that the only image thrown back by the mirror is of the woman who was looking at herself in it a moment before. Her shape, her curves and shadow dance before my eyes and prevent me from seeing what I look like myself. Myself. Myself.

The non-existent body.

She was the one who taught me this transparency: when I looked at myself I sometimes saw all of her in me, as if I had eaten her, like an apple.

She chopped onions with a sharp, thin-bladed knife. She stopped suddenly. She had cut herself. Drops of blood fall onto the table.

She raised her eyes to mine. She saw the blood, then looked at me.

The crime was now on the table, there, finely drawn in red. Then she understood. Her gaze became sharper, thrusting into me like a chisel as I stood, still motionless, on the threshold. Then it went through the kitchen wall. Into the corridor, the living room, my bedroom. It went still further, right to the end.

In an instant she saw everything: the bed; his smooth, naked body lying on top of mine, one hand over my mouth while the other grasps my wrists above my head; his knee forcing my legs apart; then him, moving rhythmically in the heavy silence of early afternoon in which not even a creak from the bed can be heard. His back glistens with sweat as he removes his hand to plant his lips on mine.

She sees everything but isn't quite sure. She is still unsure.

Why doesn't she scream, she wonders.

But it is already too late. She sees me responding to the rhythm, nothing more can ever separate us. She sees my legs open of themselves, my arms around his back.

She recognises the fingers with their short nails, tensing, gripping. Yes, it's the nails she notices. They are so different from hers: round, small, translucent pink. This image makes her close her eyes. Spectacle she cannot bear.

But she continues to watch. Nothing more can stop the inner eye that has opened in her and which penetrates beyond the reassuring surface reality, beyond appearance. She can no longer close this all-seeing eye. She knows that I will not scream, that my submission is total. She sees him roll onto his back, wrap his arms about my waist and slowly lift me on top of him. He is confident, intoxicated by the sport. From afar she sees his face, his rough lips, his half-closed eyes and the vein in his neck in which she recognises the deafening cacophony of her own pulse.

The face she is used to seeing above her, beneath her.

She feels he is looking back at her, through the walls that separate them, that he is smiling at her, remote and magnificent in his abandon. She follows the movements of his body, of his hands on the unknown lover's hips.

Then she stops.

Something in her told her to stop and look closely once more at this short-haired woman whose back is towards her. Now she recognises the graceful arch of her spine, the jutting shoulder blades and the dark patch, the size of a fingernail, in the middle. It's a birthmark, she thinks. She remembers how tiny it was when she noticed it for the first time. A scarcely-visible, golden brown mole. Like a sign. Signifying what? she wonders, then allows the question to fade from memory.

She watches me for a while, lying beside him, half-convulsed. I chew my bottom lip and stare at the wall. Then I pull the sheet over me as if suddenly I felt cold. Once more she sees the hand with its short fingernails, the same as now holds the apple core.

She stands by the table. She observes the scene in her imagination, sweating.

Again she thinks it is a product of her imagination brought on by fear. Or a dream.

She takes a mirror and, once more, checks her hair. Then her hand falls back limply as if the gesture required an exceptional effort.

Perhaps everything started that evening, on the dance floor – the question flashes through her mind: she must remember every little detail. When they met didn't he hold onto her hand for a little too long? As we were dancing didn't she stare insistently at him from a distance? 'See how she's staring at me,' he had said. She remembers blushing. Because of some vague foreboding which made her uneasy and shamed her at the same time.

Already she was ashamed for me.

Everything becomes clear to her, there, near the kitchen table, over the peeled and sliced potatoes. As, distracted, she sucks blood from her injured finger, she remembers the moment in the canoe when, for the first time, she felt her self-confidence wane. She remembers my back bent by the weight of my breasts, the look she shot out at me, betraying her fear. She understands now that there were already three of us – three at the ball, three at the breakfast table, three in the bathroom, three in the half-dark of the bedroom.

She remembers the evening when she took her transparent nightdress out of its box. She put it on without at first noticing the clumsy, semicircular hole. It was as if someone had wanted to mutilate the garment but hadn't had the patience to finish the job. When her eye finally fell on the hole in the middle of her stomach she felt its edge was hurting her, like a cut. Utterly powerless, she hid the place with her hand.

She didn't know, she didn't know how to defend herself against the violence of a child's hands rending her intimacy.

For an instant she felt defenceless, exposed to her daughter's gaze, to the stabs of her secret, stiletto hatred, visible in her ardent, anxious eyes beneath their heavy lashes, searching for evidence of their intimacy on her face, on his face. The frightened, trembling stare seemed to implore a response. 'An avowal? An explanation? Words. I know,' she thinks, 'that's what she expects from me. But I have none. I can't find any. Not even for myself.'

She remembers her hand beginning to tremble at the first breakfast we ate together, when she saw me sitting at the table wearing just my thin violet nightdress. She suddenly stopped pouring the coffee and a drop slid down the outside of the white porcelain cup. He caught it with a finger then licked it off with the tip of his tongue. It seemed to her that I had blushed all of a sudden, that I had lowered my gaze, disturbed by his gesture that revealed, more than any other, the extent of their intimacy.

One evening when we were all going out for a walk together I wanted to wear her squaw's dress, with its long zip up the back. I asked him to do it up for me. As his fingers ran up the length of my spine I closed my eyes. She saw his fingers pause on the dark fabric. She almost felt his breath on the nape of my neck. The closeness distresses her but she can do nothing against it.

Not to be frightened, not to think about it, not to let the downy trepidation invade her, deafen her.

But the fear wants out.

She feels a furtive trembling in her breast, her wildly beating heart threatens to strangle her from one minute to the next. If she opens her mouth to say anything a cloud of tiny white butterflies will swarm out and carpet the kitchen like snow. And I will discover, I will recognise her white, palpitating horror, solidifying on contact with the air.

The flakes of her anxiety form a curtain between us now, a screen woven with the succession of emerging images. She begins to tremble. I must be sick, she thinks, shivering more and more. But on the outside nothing is perceptible, nothing beyond a quickly stifled shudder.

With her hands pressed against her eyelids she heaves a scarcely-audible sigh.

We will soon be having dinner. In front of me my mother lays the table: three plates, three glasses, three forks. The smell of the roast. The television on low. She wants to calm me down before she takes any action. She is afraid for me. After the meal she will stroke my face. She will hug me. Then she will take the suitcase and fill it with the man's things. Motionless and impotent he will observe the scene that eliminates him from our lives forever.

My feet are cold and I don't dare move away from the doorway. A vague feeling of confused sadness creeps up my spine: that's not what I wanted, to hurt her. It seems to me her movements are even slower, impregnated with a senile fatigue. She bends down limply to remove the roast from the oven, then rubs the small of her back. She's lost now, but she wants to hide it. She places three knives on the table.

Light is reflected by the blade's silver cutting edge.

I recognise the sign, indicating the presence of death: death is in the air, in the three silver-bladed knives with ivory handles, in her body, in my eyes.

I didn't tell her what I saw on the pillow as his hands held me over him: her hair, spread out in a long, dark mane of snakes. With her eyes closed she tries to push them away with a shake of the head as, with a scarcely-audible hissing, the snakes flail around her face, her neck, her breasts.

It seemed to me they were binding her. It seemed to me they were whipping her.

I clearly recognised the smell of the vinegar water she uses after her shampoo – there, next to me, under me. The silk of her pale skin shone murkily, lighting the bedroom from within. As I leant over her she disappeared, melting in my hands. I felt the soft void beneath me and let myself sink without resistance into what we are, she and I at once.

I would like her to kill him. Her hands to fasten on his throat and squeeze very hard, as if it was her life

141

that was at stake, not mine. The tendons in his neck would swell up, he would open his mouth desperately for air. Still alive, the man's hands would clutch at her bruised wrists but, leaning slightly over him, she would stay calm and hold on. The same expression on her face throughout, as if absent from herself. She would continue squeezing when his face grew purple.

She would watch him die. Perceive it sensually.

Standing a little to one side, I would wait. It would take a while but I would remain utterly unmoved. I would watch for his final shudder. Then his tensed, muscular body would collapse, limply. It would no longer represent any form of danger, banal like the sleeping body of a cat.

As if carrying out some chore that couldn't be avoided she would say to me: 'Give me a hand.' I would approach. I would grasp the lukewarm legs. On the left shin I would notice a dark brown protruding mole. I would brush it gently with a finger without her seeing, but that touch would make me cry out at the top of my voice: 'No, no, no!'

The cowering desire drowned deep inside me would surge out in my voice.

To go back to my room. Wait there for night. Wait for him to slip into bed beside me and wake my half-sleeping body.

She should have killed him.

When I told her that he raped me she should have grabbed a kitchen knife, charged into the bedroom and stabbed him in the heart. Stab, then again, holding it in both hands. The long steel blade penetrating his thorax, his abdomen, diagonally into his neck. Blood flowing. Splashing on her face. But blinded by hatred and pain she would have seen only the body that had hurt her child, her little girl. Pleasure. Pain.

At one point the crime had already taken place: she was leaning over the roast as if it was his corpse, gazing at her own hands, white knuckles gripping the knife handle. She let go and it stuck into the floor.

A metallic sound softened by the wooden boards.

Again her back was to me. How graceful her neck is, I thought as my gaze slid down her spine, over the blue spotted poplin dress, her waist cinched in by a black, patent leather belt. The pleats of the dress swirling each time she moved. Now her hands kneaded the dough on the table, forward and back, regularly. She wanted to pick up the salad bowl. Her hand was white with flour. The viscous potato dough hung from her fingers but that didn't fool me. Dinner was a ruse, a trap, the preliminary to what would happen later, in the bedroom.

On her bent neck I saw the little bulges formed by her protruding vertebrae. Approach her while

her back is turned, take off her belt and strangle
her with it. In any case the belt is out of place here.
She always wears something to prove that she be-
longs to another world. That's what betrays her: her
slim waist, her pleated skirt, her shining hair, a
hidden intention in her movements.

She is completely out of place in the kitchen.

Nothing can save her from my final embrace.
Someone must pay for the dried blood on my
thighs and my belly, for the molten iron in my guts.
Her. She will pay, she will die. Not him. Since his
hands released me it's as if he no longer existed.
There is only her now, with her sharp gaze. Her,
not knowing how to talk. I wish her a painless
death, with no blood spilt on the floor. Death
creeping up behind her, like in a dream. The last
image captured by her eyes will be that of her own
floury fingers grasping the edge of the table.

Shiny black patent leather round her neck: it
must be squeezed to make the vertebrae stand out
further, stretching the skin till it almost splits.
Soundlessly. Everything must happen very quickly,
without any extraneous din. She won't have time to
utter the slightest sound. But she will want to tell
me something. 'Be quiet,' I will tell her, my hand
over her mouth. 'Don't talk. It's over. It won't take
long. No point turning your head towards me, fighting. Be calm. I don't want to see your face redden

as you struggle to escape. I don't want to see you becoming ugly. Don't make me destroy perfection . . . Oh, that skin, its softness beneath my fingers . . . Keep still!'

The belt will leave two horizontal lines, dark and ugly, as if drawn with her kohl pencil. Her lipstick will smear across her face, turning her lips into a wound. Her mascara will mix with sweat and smudge round her eyes. Her dirty, grimacing face. She will no longer be beautiful. Only the convulsions of death could obliterate her beauty.

Then she will collapse on the floor, gently, as if her body wasn't falling but wanted to lie down. I will place her head on my knees, let down her hair and smooth the wrinkled skin of her face.

Then I will plaster her with my blood.

I will drag her into her bedroom. I will lie down on the carpet next to her. There I will stay for a while, squeezed against her cooling breast. Before she becomes completely stiff I will change her, putting her into her frothy white lace dress. Under it she will be naked.

Bride in white, stripped, dead.

I will weave orange-tree flowers in her hair. I'll stick them in her mouth, in her armpits, between her thighs and toes. In the tiny shells of her ears. In her navel. On her nipples. Orange-tree shoots will sprout from her like from the earth.

Sumptuous, floral death.

I will close the window. Turn the key in the lock. For a while still the bedroom will exhale a perfume of slowly rotting flowers.

Looking at the nape of her neck I realise all at once that she is no longer just my mother. The word, the unique word that I finally uttered brought her otherness to the surface. Her other skin. She tries not to show it, makes herself busy in the kitchen to hide this other self, the bedroom self. But I know that between her experience of the body and mine there is an equals sign. I no longer have to imagine. I see her clearly in the man's arms, naked, in broad daylight. With a cold precision I feel the least of her inner movements, the slightest contraction of her muscles, the smallest shudder.

As if it was me. Now it's also me.

I see myself again at five years old, waiting in front of the locked bedroom door. I sit on the threshold. The wood smells of Ideal wax. With a grey, oblong stone I picked up in the park I scratch the door, gently, so as not to disturb her. I had fallen off the swing and grazed my knee. My fingers dabble in the mixture of sand and lymph covering the wound. It stings but I don't cry. I don't call her.

I wait for her to come out.

At first I can't hear anything. Then murmurs, laughter. Her voice gets louder, like a little silver bell tinkling in an empty, well-lit room, then softer, sighing, sobbing. I forget the pain in my knee and press my ear to the door. I tremble throughout the strangled, staccato moans. The shivering only stops when once more I hear her speak.

I am afraid for her. I know she is in danger locked in there with someone. Even when she laughs. It isn't her usual laugh, the one I know well. It's the bedroom laugh, now dark and low, now high-pitched and affected, artificial. I seem to perceive a tension in her, a frontier that must not be crossed or she will shatter, break down into sobs, tears. When I am completely calm I distinguish the voices clearly, and snatches of speech. A voice begging her: 'Let's go away together, please!' A long silence. Then her voice: 'I can't leave her.' I know she's talking about me. A trip is in the offing. She has already bought her straw hat decorated with a yellow organdie rose. When she says 'I can't' I leap up and charge into the kitchen. I lay the tea table. For them.

I set out biscuits in a bowl without eating a single one myself.

Separation, like an incision.

'I wish you were dead,' I tell her. Outside night is falling.

147

She was flabbergasted, wounded, then she sat down. With this one sentence I emptied her out, like squeezing a tube of oil paint. Finally bereft of the protection of everyday life, she seems light to me, lighter than a feather and completely unreal. I see her vacant remains looking round, imploring help in defending herself from the cruel assault, the violence she must face. But there is nothing more to be done. My words have cut her in two and suddenly she scatters.

This fragmented image of her imprints itself on my flesh as if it's the last I will ever have of her. She is seated, facing the window, grey in the setting sunlight slowly diminishing on her knees. Her hands support one another, forever alone now, subdued, ill, with their absurd, brilliantly-varnished red nails. She breathes slowly or no longer breathes at all. She doesn't move. Even her pupils are motionless.

This scene, dusk in the kitchen in the background, her on her chair in the foreground, absent, terrifying in her absence, in her inability to be here with me, slowly penetrates my body like a scalding liquid sating me till I thirst no more.

How easy it is to hate.

A pleasant heat pervades my guts, as if I'd swallowed a great gulp of some strong drink. I close my eyes. The burning sensation starts in my mouth, moves into my throat, my stomach, then little by little spreads throughout my insides: what a relief! She no longer counts either. Even before she starts talking I know that she doesn't belong here any more, that she can no longer recapture me with words, with looks, with touch.

Hatred tastes like a cooling ember.

I couldn't go on looking at her. I turned my back on her and went to hide in the bathroom. A little earlier that same afternoon he had carried me in there in his arms and put me down beneath the shower. I stood stiffly in the stream of water like a wooden statue, paralysed by fear. Not so much because of what had just happened, but because I had a premonition. I knew in advance – my body knew it more than I did – that I wouldn't keep quiet this time. This time I would have to talk to her, because what had occurred concerned both of us, her as much as me. On his knees beside the bath he soaped me with quick, jerky movements, as if he really wanted to cleanse himself of me. At one point he slowed down. He had had more than enough of my body, of the impossible, unhealthy proximity. He no longer had the strength to rinse it, to sluice off the suds of soap.

Perhaps it was only then that he understood what had happened. He stopped, looked at me, then pressed his face to my belly. Water streamed over his head, down his shoulders and back, like the hot summer rain that had completely refreshed the street outside, the roofs, the air in the bedroom and in my lungs. His shoulders shuddered and I understood that he was crying. His guilt spurted out of his eyes, his mouth. It shook him so hard that I thought he was going to die because of me, right there on the bathroom floor. I bent down and kissed his face, his eyes.

He leant his forehead against my knees; sobbing, powerless, abandoned, old. His hair was greying; there were moles all over his back. For the first time I noticed that below his waist his tanned skin was a pasty, unhealthy white. I turned away, as if I had never before seen him naked. There was something monstrous in his nakedness – in this enormous body collapsed on the edge of the bath like a corpse.

And it is a corpse, I thought, as I stood there next to him. He knows he no longer counts. No longer exists. From the way I absently run my fingers through his hair, he knows that I am elsewhere, in the space in which my mother's gaze and my own connive together, and he knows that something will happen there from which he is excluded in advance.

At that instant his lack of confidence made him vulnerable.

But now he's in the kitchen.

It is evening. They are having dinner. I hear the clatter of the cutlery and the tinkle of glasses knocking against one another. Nothing more – no voices, no words. Calmly, now, I am all ears, waiting. I am waiting for her to speak. Deep down inside I still hope, just, that she will say or do something. There is still time. It seems to me she can still get up from the table and declare: 'That's enough!' Or, right in front of him, vomit out the food she has forced herself to swallow – the soup, the potatoes, the meat, the lettuce, the wine – the living greenish porridge will stretch out across the table in a trembling mass before his disgusted eyes . . . But, through the closed bathroom door, all that reaches me is the regular, almost soporific noise of forks and knifes peacefully cutting up plates of meat. The everyday noises of dinner on Wednesday evening. Not even Sunday – Wednesday. My feeling of guilt, like some tamed animal, is already curled up on her lap. She sits. She eats. It's not her fault: from the beginning, the evening of the dance, I desired him just as much as she did. Later, every time I looked at him, every time he touched me and I said nothing, I betrayed her.

I know that she will never forgive me. She will bury my words and the image that I have caused to burst out through her bedroom wall deep down inside. She will learn to cope with it, to live with suspicion gnawing at her guts and my hatred attacking her from without.

I turned on the tap as far as it would go and let the water stream out. The noise of it covers the final message reaching me from the kitchen: It's nothing, nothing has happened.

I lie down in the bath. The water rises quickly, covering my ankles, my waist, my neck: to disappear, to melt, to metamorphose into a colourless liquid and run away down the drain. To thrust the head under and let the water penetrate the throat, the nose. To sink without resistance. Calmly. To reach the heart of nothingness.

I plunged my face into the water. I could have gone to sleep like that, never woken up, that would have been easy. At that thought I felt an immense peace pervade me, as if it had already happened. Only then did I notice that my arms and legs were trembling, like after excessive exercise. But inside I was calm – I was ridding myself of an unhealthy sediment, the last traces of an illness that persisted in places, on the surface of my skin.

I searched for something about me that might take me back in time in this state of insecurity and fear. My breasts were pert and round, my stomach firm and flat, the muscles of my legs lean and strong. My wet skin unblemished, unwrinkled, unscarred. The enamel of my teeth smooth and slippery under my tongue, free of tartar . . . In the transparent water I suddenly became aware of my body – my teeth, my nails, my hair, my eyes, my fingers, my nostrils. I felt them wholly, as if some intense, burning light illuminated them from within. Like the blinding incandescence of magnesium. This body, which a moment ago was his, belonged entirely to me now. I had conquered it for all time.

I had learnt that you have to beware of men.

And in the bath full of lukewarm water I understood that danger was founded in fear.

And that my fear was groundless. It wasn't mine. It was my mother's.

5

She carried on living with him for eight whole years. In all this time we never saw one another. I attended school in another town and lived in a hall of residence. Then I went to art school.

We phoned each other now and again. All the same, I only remember her voice vaguely – I paid more attention to the silences between the words; the way she pronounced my name; her tone as she spoke to me, the way she replaced the handset, slowly, hesitantly. Our conversations were short, circumspect, about money or my health, the sage tisane that I absolutely had to drink. We both judged it better. Forget. Forget everything.

I was forgetting.

I thought I was forgetting.

We saw each other again just three years ago. She called me from the railway station when she arrived. I said to her: 'Yes, yes. Come. Of course.' I added the 'Of course' as if to confirm – to her as much as to myself – that everything was fine now, that it was water under the bridge, that I had become an adult. 'Come.' My voice sounded calm, colourless, devoid of its usual cold caution and bitterness. The voice of a stranger, she must have thought.

I bought a watermelon for the occasion. Instead of putting it in the fridge whole and serving it in thin, semicircular slices for her to hook out the pips herself with the end of a knife, I had, unusually, cut it into cubes that I had dressed myself before arranging them in glass serving dishes.

When she came in she headed straight for a corner of the studio and sat down on a bench; she had decided beforehand not to impose on me too much by her presence. Her eye wandered round the long, half-empty, aircraft hangar of a room. It came to rest on a pile of rough timber leaning against a wall by the broad bay windows that overlooked the sunny courtyard.

'None of the things you've done are here,' she said, unsurely, scratching at the table edge with a fingernail.

'No, I don't like to keep finished work. I need space for my work in progress,' I replied, astonished I was condescending so quickly to this conversation, accepting her vocabulary.

'Things': that's how she referred to my sculptures. I didn't pick her up on it. I might easily have started explaining to her that it enabled me to clear out my internal space, that I needed that emptiness, to feel myself entirely free before attacking a new work. The emotion isn't in the eye, but in the decision: once I have taken it, I begin to weave together the strands of a new, unknown life for my material . . . But the word 'things' hung in the air between us like an invisible bridge defining our relationship, objectivising it once again.

She wouldn't have understood, I thought.

For her my sculptures are things. I don't correct her. We do not speak. We utter words which fail to reach the other, which come back to us embarrassed and a little dirty. Discouraged.

She picked up my packet of cigarettes from the table. At first she turned it over in her hands, as if about to change her mind. Then she carefully removed one from the pack and rolled it between her thumb and forefinger for a while. Shreds of tobacco spilt out on the table. She collected them up with her fingertips and dropped them into the ashtray.

'Don't worry about it,' I said.

The big wooden table was plastered with paint and turps; great creeping dark stains interconnected by scratches gouged with knives and chisels.

'It has to be done,' she said and continued to clean up the patch of table in front of her with the side of her hand.

Still just as obsessed with cleaning I thought, shuddering.

She gazed at the end of her cigarette as if to make sure it was real, then lit it and puffed a little cloud of smoke up at the ceiling. Then she leaned back against the wall and relaxed; it looked like her one moment of respite all day – all year – the moment when she finally allowed herself to pause, to lift her chin and heave a long sigh. Not of resignation. Of appeasement. Perhaps she only became conscious of the length of time that had passed when she arrived here.

She told me I had changed. My expression.

'You too . . . I didn't know you smoked.'

'No, in fact I don't,' she replied, then started to cough.

I put the bowl of watermelon on the table. As she brought the first cube to her lips it became quite clear to me what she was going to swallow along with it – bitterness, poison, particles of hate deposited inside me. It had erupted from deep within me, simultaneously with my need to prepare the fruit. I wanted to grab her hand, to stop her, to shout at her: 'No, no, no!' But her lips closed over the pink cube and it was already dissolving on her tongue.

'Isn't it sweet!' she said.

She knows, I thought. She knows she has to swallow these cubes of watermelon that I have prepared for her if she wants to see me.

I took a piece myself and bit it. The syrupy juice clung to my palate. The care I had taken could have been an expression of tenderness, but instead I could clearly taste my own recalcitrance. I wanted to demonstrate my power, even over something as futile as the pips of a watermelon. What a sublime ritual punishment: to make quite plain to her that I'm taking care of her because she has become old and impotent; peeling fruit, squeezing juice, reducing the flesh to a pap that she will bring to her mouth with a trembling hand. One or two drops will dribble down her chin: she won't even notice. Feed her with finely chopped meat, boned fish, potato purée, breadcrumbs in milky coffee: watch her toothless gums slowly, laboriously chewing the little pieces.

But she isn't old, not yet. She just has a few more wrinkles. The skin on her hands has become thinner, desiccated, but her few liver spots are hardly noticeable. In the half-light her face is distant, mysterious, still just as beautiful. She eats the cubes of watermelon with her fingers (another punishment, not allowing her any cutlery, depriving her of her habitual comforts). She is prepared for anything, even that I might spurn her and refuse all dialogue.

Beside her bed this evening I again taste the sweetness on my palate, but today it's the taste of victory.

Victory on which I gorge myself, like chocolate.

I licked my lips: they were sweet too. Perhaps it is this movement of my tongue, this sensation of pure bodily sensuality, which made me realise that finally I was satisfied. I had had enough. Her suicide attempt was enough for me. I saw her sigh heavily in her sleep and turn her head towards me. I noticed a thin trickle of saliva on her cheek.

Mechanically I wiped it away with my hand.

She looks like a child, I reflected, relieved, and the thought instantly relaxed me.

As I shut the bedroom door behind me the saliva was still wet on my palm.

It would be good if the night could last a little longer. If I could just sleep. If sleep could swallow up this tepid, viscous memory. I need time to pull myself together, to scrabble free of the quicksand of the past constantly dragging me down.

Day will soon dawn. A milky, dove grey light is already creeping into the room where objects abruptly take on an unreal appearance, as if they were made up of wraiths of mist and cloud. The bedroom is soft and round. It seems free of danger, but that doesn't fool me. I am in hostile territory, surrounded by some lurking menace, locked in a chest chock-full of objects and memories leaving no room for me.

Or for any living being.

The silence of dawn, the moment when condemned prisoners are shot.

Not a sound from behind the wall.

In the peace of the early dawn I consider for the first time that she might indeed have died. Not when I pronounced judgment, but much later, after she had taken the decision herself. The intervening years of her life have perhaps only been a sort of postponement, the time required for fully preparing herself. She had to springclean the house, discard everything still alive inside her. Everything that reminded her of life. Then there was only one thing left for her to eliminate: herself.

She sat on the edge of the bed and tipped the little white pills into a large glass of water. They dissolved slowly. Perhaps she had to stir them for a whole minute: noise of teaspoon on glass.

The only noise that morning.

Having swallowed the last mouthful of bitter, cloudy liquid, she wanted to eat something refreshing to rid her throat of the acrid taste. She got up and went into the kitchen to peel an orange. She ate two segments.

She still had so much time left.

Bitter-sweet flavour of sleep like an enormous black wave, approaching, washing over her.

The peeled orange – already a little withered – is still on the bedside table. Two segments are missing. There is a folded newspaper on the floor showing a photograph of my statue. The photograph is incredibly good. As every morning she opened her daily newspaper. She saw it, the sculpture, representing her.

Her body, annihilating everything, destroying everything around it.

I had succeeded in mastering it.

When I took her back to the railway station we had a drink in the buffet. Gooseberry juice. The train was to leave in fifteen minutes. Nervously I consulted my watch without her seeing. She twizzled her glass round and round, pensively, as if plucking up the courage to tell me one more thing before she left me. Why she came. Why she spent the entire day in a city she didn't like. Why she decided to visit me.

'Tell me something about your life.'

She blurted it out in a rush, as if she was famished and could no longer control herself.

She needed something to chew on, immediately.

That didn't surprise me, no. But I couldn't believe she had uttered those words. After a lifetime of silence. She who, whenever she spoke, had only found words that sounded false. Did she really believe I could tell her that – my 'life' – in just a few minutes? Or did she intend to miss her train and return home with me? I felt the sweat breaking out along my spine: this intrusion of tenderness was unbearable to me; like heat, it enveloped everything.

'About my life?' I said, with an effort, raising my eyebrows, as if it was something unreal. The astonishment in my voice snuffed out her final question, her sole question. It came too late.

I felt we were swapping blow for blow.

I was so used to our parallel silences. How could I tell her that my life was something flimsy and fragile that I protected with high walls, for fear someone might crush it? Tell her about myself, in my bedroom, lying in bed.

A white curtain flaps in the wind as, from a distance – it always seems to me to be from a distance

– I hear other voices, I smell baked fish, I hear a child gurgling and, distinctly, a woman's voice asking: 'Would you like to stay for dinner?' In reply the man just whistles . . . I get up at this and shut the window because I feel like a thief, a ghost absorbing the warmth of their already-sleepy voices.

I went to pay. When I got back she was still twizzling her glass with its dribble of cloudy orange juice in the bottom. I had to take her arm and help her to stand up. The train departed. It seemed to me that she was smiling furtively at me, showing that she understood my silence – as, long ago, I had understood hers. She waved goodbye. Her hand flapped and took off like a clumsy, drunken bird.

I knew she would collapse back onto her knees, abruptly powerless and excessively heavy, as soon as the train had left.

I want to see her, see her in daylight. On the balcony, leaning on the white balustrade with the blue of the sky as a background – once at least gaze at all of her, distinct. Far from the shadowy cave of this bedroom. I honestly don't feel I have ever seen her clearly, in her uniqueness. I have only seen gestures, curves, elements. Her gaze fled mine. I couldn't come close enough to her to grasp the shivers, the nuances, the shades of meaning appearing and modifying her facial expression and making her unrecognisable. There was a cruelty in the way she avoided my eye, fleeing like a winding river, some hidden obstacle diverting the current. She escaped me, still escapes me.

I seem to smell wet, freshly-turned earth in the corridor, rotting flowers – daisies, hyacinths, yellow and pink chrysanthemums. Behind the bedroom door, where I shut her in all those years ago, is a graveyard. I have to open it though. I have to.

I must have dropped off eventually. When I awoke dazzling diagonal rays of sun hatched the wall above my head. A fire engine siren rang out in the street. It's seven o'clock, I thought, as if the time of day was related to this noise. I must get going. Start of a new day.

This banal morning thought popping up behind my still-closed eyelids acts like some fresh, nourishing food, like a hot croissant with melting butter. There is something upright, something pure in this new day, a promise: the high poplar trees opposite, the gorgeous blue of the sky, the smell of toast that will soon perfume the kitchen, the first news bulletins on the radio, the weather forecast. When she wakes up all these elements will mingle within her as her bedroom becomes light and transparent, brimming with new time.

From now on everything will be different.

We will sit opposite one another like two women devoid of a past – equal, new. We will feel what very ill people must feel when they wake up after open-heart surgery that they never believed they would survive. If she's dead she'll never see what a beautiful day it is today, I thought to myself as I looked for my slippers, already convinced that she was out of danger. We should both feel reassured, safe from the past, alone at last. Her attempted suicide is a strong but invisible thread connecting us once more. The rest is unimportant – memories, men, the hard, dense feeling of abandonment, the solitude in which we are drifting.

It's because of me that she did it. It was by trying to eliminate the one thing she possessed, her body, that she finally told me, after all these years, that she loved me. As I told her that I hated her.

Neither of us needed to say a single word.

The photograph of my statue penetrates her eyes as she opens the newspaper. Pain stabbing her lungs, like lightning, then persisting. It's the first time I've made her feel anything at all. She is aware of her body torturing me still, that I have carried it within me, like a stain I am unable to wash out, throughout my absence.

She looks at the photograph and understands that inside me she slowly turned into a stone.

At last she sees her skin with my eyes.

Her marble skin.

She knows that is the true moment of her death. She feels the stone slowly growing inside her. Heaviness increasing in her legs, her belly. Her blood curdles, her movements stiffen. She knows that her eyes will remain open for some time, long enough to contemplate the white and pink mottling of the marble appearing on her legs, spreading to her bosom, her neck. Then her eyelids become heavy. Then her pupils are overtaken by a chilling, intense desire that will never again leave them.

Her hair will take longest to die.

As I got into the bath I had a peculiar sensation of being lighter than usual. I wondered if I could have lost weight overnight and the idea made me laugh out loud. I wanted to use a little bubble bath but couldn't find any: I imagined her throwing the half-empty bottle of green, pine-scented liquid into the bin in a fit of mortification.

The bath water formed shallow waves splashing on my knees and breasts. It felt like my calves were moving, that my immersed body was dissolving, becoming amorphous, unknown. I lifted a leg out of the water: it was mine after all. I thought I could hardly know myself very well to entertain such doubts. I looked closer at my leg, then scrutinised my foot. It was traced all over by wrinkles, like a cobweb. I was amazed to discover how soft and sensitive the skin was in the arch. As I explored this area of skin I realised that I didn't know my body completely, not yet, that I had been content to exist unconscious of the changes occurring to it. And all the time the wrinkles were deepening, the skin on my elbows coarsening, my nails ingrowing.

Scarcely-visible signals of my carelessness. As if for some reason I still avoided looking at myself for fear of discovering traces of injuries, of blows.

Of recognising the seat of the pain.

Of recognising the seat of pleasure.

If the most insignificant event was capable of leaving a tangible trace, my skin today would be peppered with bluish scars. But it still resists, refusing to deteriorate – I already think 'still', as, at some point, she must have done. How like her I am as, immersed in the hot water, I scarcely feel my own weight. I seek out changes in myself, evidence of withering time. Once more the certitude, the recognition from within: I am inside her, under her skin, cowering in her guts. I am convinced that words are unable to describe this condition in which we form one, this osmosis between two identical beings.

Immersed in the hot water I know now that I will be able to forget everything. What happened inside becomes transparent, fluid, like the bluish water. The years gone by have left me just a memory of sand and mud, of my hands digging into clay, of my hands, of the clay. The desire to model, like a need, like hunger. Forms which I absorb which then burst out again when I think I have forgotten them. Sharp shadows thrown by trees in moonlight, light refracted from the wall opposite. Smell of wood: shavings still moist with sap curling away from my chisel. I feel so close to myself that a new space, a hollow, opens up inside me. Somewhere deep in my stomach I have the pleasant sensation of something moving, gently stirring; yearning for cossetting tenderness, yearning for a child.

But the thought remains a tiny spot on the edge of my consciousness; I can't catch hold of it.

Not yet. Not now.

While I am drying myself I notice how strong my arms are, the muscles in my legs firm and taut, as if I was about to run off somewhere. I feel ready to accomplish some exploit. The word *new* runs through my mind several times though I know it's not the right one. When I taste the sharp minty toothpaste on my tongue I realise the right word is *present*.

In the bedroom the morning is completely different – dark and suffocating.

As soon as I opened the door I was choked by a stench of rot and airlessness rising from the darkness

– the smell of withered flowers whose stems have rotted to mush. I noticed a great bouquet of faded anemones in a vase on the commode. Through the transparent glass I saw a green film had coated the inside of the vase. I drew back the curtains, opened the window and raised the awning. Street cleaners had just sluiced the road and the dust rising from the wet asphalt penetrated the room simultaneously with the sun.

The whole bedroom shone with a grainy glow.

The light curled up in the centre of the carpet like a great, bright, silver animal, transforming the room from within.

Until now it had seemed familiar to me. So familiar it made me uneasy perhaps. I knew the furniture by heart, their smallest details: the walnut commode containing bedlinen, the huge wardrobe with carved doors and a mirror inside, the armchair, the oval dressing table with its old-fashioned glass bottles of beauty products, the double bed.

It was her bedroom, the bedroom on the other side of the wall.

But in the harsh light the objects suddenly took on a new appearance. It was as if I had never seen them before or as if they had become worn: I noticed the holes in the lace curtain and how it was black with dirt around the gathers. The edge of the white silk covering the dressing table was a greyish yellow.

The glass chandelier no longer hung from the centre of the plaster ceiling rose. One of the wardrobe's hinges was broken and a paler wood was visible where a piece of metal had come away. I sat down in the armchair: the green fabric on its arms was threadbare. So as not to have to dust it she had hidden the sewing machine behind the door with a nylon cover over it, but the cover was already grey with dust and torn in several places. The edges of the rug were frayed. The shade on the bedside lamp was scorched on one side.

I approached the bed.

On the headboard was a triangle of three little black holes. As if someone had tried several times to knock a nail in before giving up. They were so prominent that my head immediately began to ache.

Wherever I look. Wear. Dilapidation of the things that used to surround me, disgusting me at first, then making me queasy. These objects covered with their dull patina were no longer in their proper places; already they were sinking into non-existence.

Her gaze failed to take in the dust, the holes, the ragged carpet, the imperfections, harbingers of decomposition. It struck me that nothing more would be required to sort out her room – to sort out her life. She lay surrounded by ruins. In some corners nettles had already taken root and mould was creeping across the walls. She lay there peacefully, abandoned.

I sat down on the bed close beside her. At eye level on the wall I noticed the tiny trace of a squashed, mummified mosquito. Heaven alone knew how long it had been there. Years perhaps. On the white wall, just above her head. Smear of dried blood with little wings sticking out. She didn't notice it, paid it no heed – the blood didn't disturb her. Her eyes, clouded by a fine mist, no longer noticed such trifles. In any case, she wouldn't have been able to halt the process of decomposition that took objects over, the time that devoured them. She had no alternative but renunciation.

All around me in this bedroom with its naked walls I could see evidence that the process of her giving up on life had already been going on for years and that nothing would now ever be able to halt it.

I was sitting close beside her. She was still asleep and her eyes flickered from time to time behind her fine, rather wrinkled eyelids. She would soon wake up. Her breathing was slow and peaceful. Her hands rested on the bedspread, palms upwards. Her wrists were delicate with protruding bones and veins along which the pulsing blood was scarcely visible.

How I love her sleeping, feeble hands. Her damp, gentle palms, concave like welcoming little nests. Her long, ringless fingers. The way she held her cigarette that time in my studio – rather stiffly, as if she still needed practice. The way she waved good-bye when we parted.

I tried to hold back my tears but couldn't. I cried so much the tears seemed to come not from my eyes but from my throat, or from deeper still, the shadowy hollows way down inside me in unknown regions of my body where for so long they had been accumulating. I thought I had no more tears. But they flowed out of me, running down my cheeks, my neck, my breasts. At first I cried silently, with short, strangled sobs, then louder and louder until my voice wrenched itself from me like an avalanche.

I think I started bawling. I don't know how loud or for how long. I was wailing as if she was already dead. Or as if the new things that had sprung up between us were dying – the light on the carpet, the transparent morning, the taste of mint, the future. A wild, unknown cry relieved me of my solitude. It rose to the ceiling, went out through the window and the door, echoed in the corridor, bouncing off the walls. The cry was so powerful that it deafened the whole town. Ricocheting between the buildings and the canopies of the trees, it flew back to me and I had to swallow it once more. Shut up inside me once again it turned into a whine. Curled up on the floor next to the bed, softly wailing.

'Don't cry.'

Her hand on my face.

She was lying on the very edge of the bed, stroking me with her fingertips. Brushing against me like a gust of wind, a magical touch erupting from the distant past, when I would wait for her, in bed, before closing my eyes, alone in the shadows of childhood.

She didn't come. I don't remember her ever coming.

'Shush, stop now, it's all right, everything will be fine.'

Her calming voice covers me like a blanket. Sleep clouds my eyes. Just before I let go I see her again at the railway station, standing at the door to the carriage in her grey skirt and delicate white blouse. She hangs on to the handle with one hand. With the other she scrunches up her handkerchief. She leans forward a little as if she has something important to tell me.

'Take good care of yourself,' she murmurs, quiet as can be.

I do not reply. I stand on the platform in the bright sunlight. She is in shadow. From this distance she still looks absolutely fine. But I am frightened that if I approach I will see the solitude corroding her face. The train departs. She is alone, a pale smear in the darker frame of the door.

On my way back the rays of the setting sun lengthened and almost made it possible to distinguish individual grains of dust on the blue canvas awning outside the office supplies shop. There is so much dust you just don't see, I thought, turning into the road which led to my home.

It can't have lasted long, perhaps an hour. Then I woke up. The bedroom seemed the same but there was no longer her hand hanging over the edge of the bed. I stood up and saw that she too had gone back to sleep. Propped up by pillows with her mouth half open, she slept with her head resting on her right shoulder. Her sleeping face was at once fragile and haggard, as if it had shrunk.

Fear she will be cold if I touch her.

I immediately stretch out a hand: the skin on her face is hot, a little soft. She blinks. Then she smiles, embarrassed, as if apologising for falling asleep at the wrong moment – yet another clumsy gesture pushing her further away from me. I bring her a glass of water. She drinks it in long, greedy swallows. Wipes her mouth with the back of her hand, leans back on the pillows and covers her eyes with her arm.

'It's so bright,' she says. 'It hurts my eyes.'

'Do you want me to lower the blinds?'

'No, no!' Her voice is a little thick because of the rubber tube they thrust into her when they pumped her stomach.

Her upper body is exposed now. She is still wearing the thin, spotted, flannelette hospital nightdress. It has no buttons and gapes open on her chest. The arm stretched across her eyes trembles slightly. I can see a bruise inside her elbow, where they put in the drip – the nurse must have had two or three goes at it to find the vein. Finally she lowers her arm as if she too needed time to get used to the bedroom's new appearance. She pushes back the bedspread and sits up. Then, leaning on the bedside table, she tries to get up. She stands there in her bare feet in the crumpled, outsize nightdress that hangs down to her knees. With her left hand she holds it shut across her breasts – not to hide them from me but as if she felt a draught and was suddenly cold.

She can't take a single step and flops back down on the bed. I lift her legs back up and straighten the pillows.

'I'll bring you some water to get cleaned up,' I tell her.

She looks at me. Runs a hand through her hair: a few shining white ones can be seen between her fingers. It's like the holes in the curtains, I thought, at first you don't see them. She says nothing. Her lips are pale, almost white, dry and cracked. I place the bowl on her knees. She washes, slowly: scooping up a little water in the hollow of her hand and bringing it towards her face requires an effort that is almost beyond her. She lets herself fall back onto the pillows without even getting dry. The water trickles down her cheeks, soaks into her hair, moistens the collar of her nightdress. I wipe her face and hands. Her eyes are closed. One more thing requiring an effort of which she is at present incapable: confronting the world once again. She still seems undecided to me, that she hasn't yet crawled up out of the black hole that swallowed her a few days ago, that my presence is disturbing her, that the light is blinding her, that the venomous weight of her own body is crushing her.

She even breathes weariness.

I change her clothes, without a word. I take the dreadful nightdress off her – that detritus smelling of waiting rooms, hospital, chlorine, disinfectant, thin soup thickened by a few meagre strands of vermicelli. I dip the corner of a towel in lukewarm water and start to wash her. Her back first. She sits leaning forwards. I feel her ribs and vertebrae beneath my fingers. She's thin, I think, cleaning her even more meticulously, to scrub away this deposit, to purify her, to break through to her, her clean, white skin. She leans back on the pillows. She is completely exposed, abandoned to my gaze.

It's the first time I have seen her naked breasts so close up.

I stop. My hands holding the wet towel stop in mid-air. A drop of water falls on her naked belly but she doesn't move. She waits. I feel I haven't the right to touch her. No, not now. It's absolutely out of the question. Something unpredictable might happen. Desire, so long repressed, still throbs inside me and might burst forth.

Thirst for her body that I feel through my fingertips.

The image that tortures me reappears: I see her lying on the bed one hot, stormy afternoon. She is naked, lying on her side. Light lingers on her golden skin.

I see her turning over in her sleep.

I see the man's hand rest upon her.

My own, undecided, still holds the towel.

A second drop of water falls on her belly. But now it's another woman. Between her breasts I see the little dent that her thinness has hollowed in her thorax. As my hand at last approaches her breasts I become aware of how much time has passed – how her body has softened, as if squeezed into this hollow between her breasts: fine white stretch marks have appeared on her sides; her stomach muscles and thighs have become flaccid, her skin has lost its shine.

This body is disintegrating.

My fingers become lost in the slack, limp flesh infected by age.

Simultaneously I feel tenderness and disgust.

She doesn't move, doesn't pull up the sheet. She lets me stare at her, have my fill of her, as if she knew that my eyes are my consciousness and that I can only understand the changes time has wrought in her by drinking her in with my gaze. I lay my head on her belly. How I wanted to do just this so long ago! Feel her skin on my face. Her smell would have chased away all my fears.

Sink. Fuse absolutely with this feeling of presence, of finitude.

I understand now that only the distance separating us could beget my sculpture, the obstacles, my inability to approach her. The image graven on my memory was refracted by desire.

Obsession, blindness: see only one aspect of her, for years carry around inside me a petrified matrix, defining me utterly. What was I hoping for? That by bringing it out into the open I might discover the meaning of my work – which is just a projection of myself? That I would understand the meaning of that statue I exhibited, that petrified beauty still dominating me?

It seems to me that I have two mothers now, one that I have lost leaving only a trace in the marble, and another one, alive, whose face has just peeked out from behind the broken stone mask.

Resting on her belly I suddenly remember a description of the way marble degrades that I read years ago in the *Restorer's Manual.* As time passes the stone takes on the appearance of saccharose, its crystals disintegrate, the statue's corners become worn, wind and rain wear it away like a sand dune.

Her face seems eaten away by leprosy.

It's as if I had sculpted her a thousand years ago. My mother is emerging from beneath the decrepit, powdery stone.

There she is before me, revealed at last. Fresh scars of her former beauty are still appearing, but it is no longer relevant, neither to her nor to me.

I am close to her at last.

When, a little later, she left the bedroom, did I open the drawer of the bedside table? What was I looking for? The thermometer, pills, the prescription the doctor left yesterday evening? Or was I still suspicious? Did I still feel she was hiding something from me, something I knew about by instinct: a little piece of her, curled up, shuddering, shivering, condemned never to see the light of day? Once the drawer was open it was too late. Inside I saw a little photograph album I had never seen before, although it was very old, as was obvious from the worn leather cover with its threadbare corners. As I took hold of it a photograph fell out. I picked it up. I held it for a moment in my hand, not under-standing. Bizarre . . . There was something at once peculiar and staggering about it. I turned it towards the light: where the face should have been was a hole the size of a fingernail.

The faceless man was my father.

She was standing beside him. His arm was around her shoulders, pulling her towards him. She was smiling, her head tilted towards his, in a black dress with little white spots. They were in a town square with pigeons fluttering round their ankles, a great mass of pigeons. Venice, of course. I recognise the church in the background. Ice creams. Cappuccino in the shade of a Renaissance palace. Gondolas. Summer. I wasn't yet born but perhaps I already existed under the spotted fabric that clung to her belly, perhaps moving inside her on the sunny piazza where some faceless, nameless person had captured her smile with the camera.

My father wore long white trousers, a short-sleeved shirt and a Panama hat. In his right hand he held his glasses. Why had he taken them off? Was it to look younger standing next to her? More handsome for her? With his tanned arms he seemed relaxed in the company of this woman who leaned her body against his. Among a thousand faceless bodies he would have known hers, among a thousand perfumes only hers intoxicated him, among the smells of the canal, the cafés, the roads leading from the piazza San Marco on this summer day in 195 . . .

What expression was there on his face? Was it the suspicious half-smile so typical of him? Or could he still smile openly, as if he trusted the world around him, the pigeons, the bell-tower, the sky: the firm, magnificent body wrapped around his? As I look at him he becomes a ghost-person, his Panama overhanging a black hole eternally sucking him in.

Once again the insidious internal assault, beating against the walls of my veins. A dangerous, burning liquid threatens to erupt like lava. Rage making me want to lash out, to break things, shatter them to pieces, to bite. What has she done? What has she done? Why, instead of his face, is the only thing left me my palm, seen through the hole in the photo-graph – this pale, impersonal blotch which makes me feel even more nauseous?

She's insane, completely insane. It's a warning. I mustn't open the album. I'm bound to discover the most crushing evidence that will drive me away from her once more. But these fingers are already opening the cover, turing over the dark grey cardboard pages.

The pages are empty. The photos are all stacked up between the last page and the back cover. She must have torn them out (here and there the surface of the cardboard is torn) then sorted them into an order only she understands. There aren't many, perhaps twenty. Several of them are of my father. The others of men I don't know. Most show her alongside the man from the dance, my ex-stepfather, her ex-husband.

Not a single one of the men has a face.

Faceless, lipless, eyeless bodies. I recognise them through details – their clothes, their shoes, their hair or some characteristic gesture. I identified my father by his watch and glasses like a disfigured corpse at the morgue. I can see the next photograph through the oval hole. Fragments of a hand or a landscape, a piece of her face.

A smell of blood. A sweetish, familiar fragrance that impregnates her as she cuts out their faces, as she robs them of their identities, reducing them to an empty circle, to nothingness.

A hole in space. Absence.

I see her sitting on her bed late one night. As many times before she takes the album from her drawer. It's unpremeditated. She has just woken from a disturbed sleep and in the darkness cannot dispel her anxiety. She turns on the bedside lamp. She looks at the photographs, glued, sorted. It gives her an impression of order, that there is a reason for everything, more or less. For a moment she feels less alone. But she looks at them for too long. She scrutinises them as if scraping away the layers of forgetfulness one by one. The faces eventually come alive in her memory. Abruptly she sinks into their embrace, recaptures the taste of their lips. She relives certain conversations, certain dances. Their steely eyes grate across her skin, captivating her. Desire comes alive again inside her. She contemplates the whirl of smiling faces, lips murmuring promises, hands gripping her waist, her shoulders. Then she sees her own solitude lying on the pillow next to her. She has only to reach out a hand and touch it. She can hug it, feel it penetrating her, filling her up. Now she is inside, right inside her own body, somewhere between her breasts and her stomach, deep inside. Her throat is dry. She no longer has a choice. When she breathes deeply she feels loneliness entering her blood. 'I am trapped,' she thinks. 'This loneliness will never leave me.' Her throat is dry, but there is no help.

She peels the photographs away one by one. Some of them resist. She pulls harder. The noise of tearing paper lacerates her eardrums. She stops, unsure it seems, but perhaps she isn't hesitating. In fact it's at that precise moment that she must have decided to take from the same bedside drawer her manicure set in its long red case. She gets out the nail scissors. The short steel blades mutilate the first picture. The paper is brittle with age – thirty years, twenty, ten ... Time winds in a spiral beneath her hand in the whisper of the steel blades.

The task engrosses her. Carefully she cuts around the shapes of the faces. Sometimes they are very small and that makes it difficult. At one point she considers cutting their heads off completely – in one photograph you can see the incision where she sent the scissors towards the hair and ears – but she returns to the line marking the edge of the face and follows it right to the end, meticulously. It's as if her life was spread out in front of her in each stiff rectangle of card. She rejects everything that displeases her, that part of herself that she despises.

She tries to convince herself that it is possible to eradicate these faces from her past.

Only their bodies will remain. Soon she will no longer be able to tell them apart. Deprived of their identities they will disappear, precipitated like a sediment at last in the depths of her memory.

As she cuts she feels an insidious, constant pain in her thorax – the empty space. That doesn't stop her, though. She slices through the photographs

184

one after another as if obliged to excise the hard, painful lumps and nodules that have invaded her flesh. She destroys them. Slowly, insolently annihilates them. Then she collects up the tiny faces scattered across the bespread and burns them in the ashtray with a small blue flame. The dry paper is consumed incredibly quickly. In the end the flat-bottomed container contains just a little ash and a few blackened, withered twists that collapse into powder at the slightest touch.

For a short while before going back to sleep she smells the burnt paper.

I take up the picture of my father on the piazza San Marco once more. Through the rounded oblong hole that used to contain his face I distinctly see my mother's despair, her solitude, the void in which she is sinking. By cutting holes in her own body, digging into the past, she cut a pathway through to the darkness beyond. I lift the photograph up to the light. Through the opening a little sky and window are visible. Then her face alongside. She is alive. She alone is alive. I know now that there is no way of reaching any deeper inside her, no way of reaching her solitude; or the feeling that forced her to admit her solitude to herself that night, and to accept it.

Examining the ruins more closely – her bedroom ravaged by the light, her body deformed by time, her despair visible through the oval apertures in the photographs – I understand that she had to make the best of it. She tried but couldn't. Now she will have to try again.

So, she didn't give a thought to me, I said to myself, gazing at the obliterated faces. But no. In fact it was the only way she could reach me. She had to drive them all out. Renounce them all.

It had cost her a great deal to strip herself of that which was most important to her and visit me. And she had come. She had eaten the cubes of watermelon saturated with bitterness and thought: There's no point. It's hopeless. I've lost her too. She had looked at me through the carriage window as I stood on the platform, motionless, stubborn. I still wore my hair short, my hands thrust deep in the pockets of my jeans. I shrugged, defensively.

Her face is pinched, she thought, irritated, afraid. She's afraid I will hurt her with my clumsy speeches, with the questions I don't know how to ask. Words, words, words. I can see in her face that she's had enough, in the way she studies my every gesture, her silence just now as we drank. She can't be bothered. I came too late. Too bad. At least I tried.

How tiny she is, tinier and tinier. The red smudge of her hair becoming more and more distant on the platform. Inaccessible.

186

She thinks perhaps she will never see me again.
She waves once more, in case I can still see, even
though the train has already left the station.

Back home she gazes at the photographs of me as
a child hung on the wall. Then she shuts the bedroom door again quietly, as if I still lived there and
was sleeping.

A few moments ago I thought I was going to leap
on her when she came back in, shove the photograph album into her face and ask her why she did
it – why, why, why? But it's not the right question.
It's no longer the right question.

Image of the scissors in her hands.

Image of the scissors in mine: what pathetic
weapons we turn to in secret to defend ourselves
from the emptiness around us!

I won't ask her anything. I'll put the album back
in the drawer without even mentioning it to her. We
will sink into silence together once more, a silence
that will not last – just twenty-four hours, till tomor-
row, perhaps a few days. We will say nothing until we
are sure we are able to talk of something else. Not
be forced to speak of ourselves. Because otherwise
we would ask each other questions to which there is
no answer: voices careering away from meaning. We
would become bogged down in the past – in our
respective guilts, in inextricable darkness.

I will be content to nurture a new image inside me: her despair. I am already conscious that this is the beginning of a new era, the thread that will lead me back to myself and to sculpture. As others recognise hunger or thirst, I can recognise the moment when dumbness becomes speech – that particular kind of language.

'A coffee would be nice,' she says to me, gaily.

She goes back into her bedroom, her hair shining, wearing a long satin dressing gown, transformed.

In the kitchen, at the back of the crockery cupboard, I find the old espresso machine. So she didn't throw it out! I think, delighted.

And when I swallow a mouthful of freshly-made coffee, I know that forgiveness, like the warm, aromatic liquid itself, will slip conclusively down my throat.